SPIKE

BURNING SAINTS MC BOOK #6

USA TODAY BESTSELLING AUTHOR
JACK DAVENPORT

2023 Jack Davenport
Copyright © 2023 Trixie Publishing, Inc.
All rights reserved.
Published in the United States

Spike is a work of fiction. Names, characters, places, and incidents are the products of the author's imagination and are used fictitiously. Any resemblance to actual events, locales, or persons, living or dead, is entirely coincidental.

Cover Art
Jack Davenport

TRIXIE
PUBLISHING

ISBN: 9798386628550

Printed in the USA
All Rights Reserved

PRAISE

BURNING SAINTS

Oh, good gravy, this book is good. And I'm not just saying that because he does other amazing things with his fingers!
~ **Piper Davenport, Contemporary Romance Author**

Piper
I couldn't do any of this without you. Literally, my fingers would fall off and I'd be a vegetable.

Liz Kelly
You are truly one the greatest humans on the planet. Thank you so much for all your amazing insights!

Brandy G.
Thank you for the million reads and your attention to detail!!! You're amazing.

Gail, Mary, Carrie, and Trudy
Thank you for all your help

For my real-life Trixie

You have been my fascination, my inspiration, my muse, and true love since the day I met you.

I can't imagine my life without you, and look forward to each new day with you. Thank you for inviting me along on this crazy ride.

ONE

BURNING SAINTS

Spike

Six years ago…

THE VAN PULLED up to Ridge Park High School and we quickly filed out and lined up. Our group of twelve were all too familiar with the rules and weren't about to risk our walking papers over lack of following proper procedure.

"Gentlemen," Sergeant Hopper bellowed. "I'd like to remind you that we are guests here tonight and that you'd all better be on your best behavior or Mr. Fields will be more than happy to drive us all home early. Is that understood?"

"Yes, sir," we responded in perfect unison.

"Good, because if a single one of you steps as much as an inch over the line tonight, you'll *all* catch extra time."

"Yes, sir," I said, making sure my voice was loud and clear.

My release date was exactly twenty-seven days away. All I had to do was toe the line and be a good little robot and I'd be free in less than a month. I had no idea what that freedom would look like, but I knew it was free of curfews, beatdowns, guards, inmates, and forced labor. At least that's what my young, dumb ass thought at the time.

We walked in a single file line, eyes set straight ahead as Hopper led us to the gym. As we made our way through the campus, I spied everything I could. Taking as many mental snapshots as possible. Storing them away in my memory until I had the opportunity to write everything down in my journal. The walls were lined with rows of lockers, painted in alternating green and white. Vending machines filled with everything from snacks and sodas to pens and notebooks were scattered throughout. The school was old, but well maintained, and somehow cheery, even at night. This was the type of school where I should have spent the last four years, but instead I'd been enrolled in the Lakewood Youth Correctional Center, courtesy of a hard-ass judge and Portland's shittiest public defender. My education came to me in the form of beatings, hustles, systemic indifference, and legal travesties. When the world was trying to teach me some sort of lesson, I was educating myself. I read everything I could get my hands on. From Covey's Seven Habits of Highly Effective People to Kipling's Seven Seas. When I wasn't reading, I was writing in my journal. Something my mom had encouraged me to do for as long as I could remember.

Arriving at the gym, Hopper took one more opportunity to address us, this time a little less formally.

"Now, look boys. This will be the first time some of you will have seen a girl in person in quite a while and I'd better not see any foolish behavior from any of you. You are to keep your powder dry at all times. No fighting over who dances with who, and no advances, sexual or otherwise. The young ladies that are here tonight are good, clean, Christian girls, and with the help of their church, have put this evening together for you. Don't go spoiling it for them."

"Yes, sir," we replied, once more.

"With that, enjoy your night and your first taste of freedom, but remember that I and the chaperones will have our eyes on you."

Sergeant Hopper opened the double doors and the sight of the gym just about brought tears to my eyes. It was the first time I'd even come close to crying for years, and I was thankful that the rest of the group were also too busy gawking at our surroundings to notice. The gym had been completely transformed into a California beach scene, complete with a volleyball net and real sand which covered every square inch of the gym except for the dance floor. Even though I was born in a coastal state, I'd never been to a real beach before. My mom took me to the shore once, when I was five years old, but the beach was covered with rocks and driftwood, the water was freezing cold, and the wind gusts were so high, they'd knock me on my ass. I was miserable and did nothing but cry and moan the entire time. I've never gone back to one of our so-called "beaches" since and have always dreamed of seeing the Pacific Ocean from the shores of Southern California. For now, this would do nicely.

A band, made up of teenage guys and girls, played Fifties-style instrumental surf music on a stage at one end of the room, and on the other was a large grill, loaded up with hamburger patties and hot dogs. Styrofoam coolers stocked with sodas, chips, and cookies were nestled into the sand throughout the "beach." I thought I'd died and gone to heaven. Our diet back at the House was very restricted and regimented. It was high cuisine next to what they flung at us back at Lakewood, but still nothing like this.

Our group was made up entirely of "long timers." Inmates who'd been at Lakewood for three years or more. Besides my bunkmate "Screek," who'd been inside for almost five years, I was the next most senior member of the House.

Inmates who do their time, without stirring up too much shit, got to serve their last six months as a resident of the Lakewood Resident or 'the House' as it was known to us. The house was a minimum-security halfway house that was more like a youth hostel than prison. We cooked and ate our meals together, did all the household chores as a group, and even got to watch a movie on Saturday nights. Sergeant Hopper lived onsite and monitored every move we made. Mr. Fields, or 'Fieldy' as we called him, was our driver, handyman, babysitter, or whatever else Hopper told him to do. He played it straight around the boss but was always cool to us. Sometimes he'd sneak in junk food or slip in a movie that wasn't on the approved list. We were still incarcerated, but the House was pure luxury compared to gen pop at Lakewood.

Screek elbowed me while pointing to a large banner that read, "Lifesprings Church welcomes you."

"How welcoming you think these church girls really are?"

"I swear to whatever God these people believe in I will strangle you in your bunk tonight if you get us bounced out before I get to eat at least three burgers," I replied.

"Welcome, gentlemen," a middle-aged woman with bright red hair said as she approached. "We're so happy and honored to have you as our guests this evening. I know the students are all very excited to meet you and celebrate your upcoming... *graduation.*"

"Thank you for inviting us Mrs. Mitchell," Sergeant Hopper said. "Our boys are going to be on their best behavior tonight."

"Of course, they will," she said cheerily. "And please call me Sherri."

"Will I get the chance to see your husband tonight?"

"No, I'm sorry," she said, almost singing her response. "Pastor is in Tacoma, attending a conference and won't be back until tomorrow night, just before evening services."

Screek leaned in and whispered, "Did she just call her husband 'pastor'?"

I shrugged, equally as confused as he was.

Besides never stepping foot on a decent beach, the soles of my shoes had never crossed the threshold of a church before, and even though this was a school gymnasium, it was clear we were currently standing on holy ground. Or at the very least, Lifesprings Church ground.

"Please, boys, come and get something to eat and drink. Our students are ready to serve you."

I wasn't sure what she meant by students, but all became clear as we neared the grill. Standing behind a row of large folding tables was a line of kids who looked to be our age. Most of them girls. They all wore matching black T-Shirts with bold white lettering which read 'Lifesprings Church Student Ministries.' Each kid also wore a nametag, not that it mattered much. Most of them, boy or girl, seemed to be named Logan, Bailey, or Jordan.

We were each given a tray which held two plates a

cup and plastic silverware. Moving down the chow line felt a little like being back at Lakewood, but the food and some of the servers sure looked a hell of a lot better. They all said things like 'bless you,' and 'thank you for joining us tonight,' as they cheerily shoveled macaroni salad and baked beans onto our plates.

After grabbing some burgers and dogs, Screek scoped us out a table and we took our seats. Both of my plates were piled high, and I could barely wait to dig in when another student walked in and took her place behind the dessert station.

She had long blonde hair and the brightest blue eyes I'd ever seen. She smiled wide as her friends greeted her and I momentarily forgot how to breathe. I always thought that was some sort of corny expression, someone taking your breath away, but I swear, for at least thirty seconds, I fucking forgot how to inhale and exhale.

"You, okay, bro?" Screek asked.

"Uh, ah, yeah. I, uh, ahhh," I stammered. "I…I…I'm gonna go get some dessert."

Bolting from my seat I heard Screek call out, "You haven't even started eating your dinner!"

I pushed my way through my fellow housemates, practically flinging myself toward the dessert station.

"Uh, hi," the blonde said, with a sweet, but surprised giggle.

"Hi, hello…um. I'd love some, uh, dessert, please," I said, studying her face. She was the most beautiful girl I'd ever seen.

"Oh, I'm not quite set up," she said, tying her apron. "Sorry, I just got here. Besides, everyone is sitting down for dinner."

"Yeah, I'm not really that hungry," I said.

She pointed at the empty spot next to Screek, who was staring directly at us. "Are you sure? Because, from here,

6

it looks like your tray is pretty full."

"Oh, that's not my tray…well, it *is* my tray, but it's my *dinner* tray, and I always like to eat dessert first, so I'm gonna save all that food until afterwards."

"Dessert first, huh?" She raised an eyebrow. "Doesn't that spoil your appetite?"

"No, not at all. Of course not," I replied, noticing she wasn't wearing a name tag.

"How do you manage that?"

"Listen," I said leaning in. "I'll let you in on a secret my mom told me when I was a little kid."

"I love secrets," she replied, ducking her head down lower.

"I had a feeling I could trust you," I said.

She stifled a laugh and I quickly had to remind myself to breathe again.

"Okay," I whispered. "When I was eight years old, my mom leveled with me. She told me that grownups lie to their kids about dessert spoiling their appetites."

"Really?"

I nodded. "Parents only tell kids that story so they can use dessert as a reward mechanism for their children to clean their plates. They don't want children to know the *real truth*."

"What's that?"

"That the human stomach has a meal chamber and a dessert chamber."

Her mouth formed a small 'O' shape and then she smiled again. "Stomach chambers? Like a cow?"

"Yes, indeed. And even if one of them is full, there is still room in the other. So, it really doesn't matter which you eat first."

"I see. And you prefer dessert first?"

"Of course. What if something horrible happens midway through and this wonderful meal is brought to an untimely end? I'd regret not coming over here and at least trying the dessert you worked so hard to make."

"It's ice cream," she said, pointing to the commercial-sized store-bought chocolate and vanilla. "In a tub."

"Sure, it is, but I bet you're an amazing scooper outer."

She rolled her eyes. "Let's go back to the horrible thing that's going to happen before dessert."

"Oh, I didn't say it *was* going to happen, only that it *could* happen."

She settled her hands on her hips and smirked. "Like what kind of horrible thing?"

I shrugged. "I don't know. An earthquake, a hurricane, avalanche, flood, plague of locusts. Hey, that sounds like a Bible story."

She chuckled. "That's true."

"Oh, wait, what about the rapture? When all the good people are taken up to heaven. I'm sure you'd be one of them. What if the rapture happens and you got sucked up to heaven and left me here on Earth before I ever got to witness your sick scooping skills."

"You've clearly got the end times all figured out. Do you read the Bible a lot?"

"Not so much, but Saturday is movie night at the House, and one time we watched this one with some guy named Kurt Cameron about the rapture. It sucked, but I guess all that shit's in the Bible, right?" My hand went to my mouth. "Oh, shit. I'm sorry. I didn't mean to swear in front of you."

She smiled wide. "I've heard the word *shit* before."

Even the way she cursed was adorable. She may have heard the word, but I wasn't convinced she'd ever said it until now.

"And I think it's *Kirk* Cameron that was in the first Left Behind movie."

I gasped. "The *first* one? Someone made sequels to that movie?"

She held up four fingers. "Four movies in total. Nicholas Cage is in the latest one."

I stared at her blankly. "I have no response to that."

Her jaw dropped. "What did you say?"

"Nothing," I said, dismissively. "I just said, I have no response to that. It's a quote from—"

"Joe Versus the Volcano?"

"You've *seen* that movie?" I asked in complete disbelief.

"It's my favorite movie of all time."

"That's impossible," I said.

"We're only allowed to watch PG and G movies in my house, and that was one we owned. It barely made the cut because of the kissing, but dad said it was okay because they get married. I watched it so many times, my brothers eventually hid the DVD from me."

Joe Versus the Volcano was a romcom released in nineteen ninety starring Tom Hanks and Meg Ryan. It's about a guy who's a total loser who agrees to jump into an active volcano to save an island of people who are obsessed with orange soda. The movie was a box office bomb and is hardly ever talked about. By anyone but me.

I rolled up my sleeve and showed her my forearm which bore my first tattoo. It was a crooked, inverted lightning bolt within a triangle. A recurring and highly significant symbol within the movie.

She gasped and covered her mouth. "Is that real?"

"Got this two years ago. See that funny looking guy over there that keeps gawking at us?"

She nodded.

"That's my best friend, Screek. He's crazy, but he's also a crazy talented artist."

"His name is Screek?"

"Well, his real name is Dawson, but I started calling him Screek, because…"

She smiled wide. "I get it. Dawson… Screek…Dawson's Creek."

"Beautiful *and* smart," I said, causing her to blush immediately.

"Are all your references from the nineties?"

"We have a limited library at our house too," I said, rebuttoning my sleeve cuff.

"What's your name?" she asked, beating me to the punch.

"Spike."

"Spike? And what's *that* nickname in reference to?"

"Who said it's a nickname?"

She bowed apologetically. "You're right. Spike could be your birthname. Your mother does sound like she's pretty cool. I mean, she did level with you about the dessert chamber."

I forced a smile and nodded. "She was very cool."

Her hand went to her mouth. "Oh, I'm sorry I—"

"It's okay," I said, quickly. "She passed a few years ago, but she'd been sick a long time."

"Now I kind of have to give you ice cream, don't I?"

"I believe it is proper dead mother etiquette, to serve refreshments while speaking of the departed," I said, causing her to laugh so hard she snorted.

"Oh, my gosh, that's horrible," she said.

"She would have laughed right along with you. Maybe not the snorting part."

She blushed. "Okay, back to the original subject, Spike, which is it? Nickname or real name?"

I smiled. "I'll tell you, if you'll agree to dance with me."

"No one else is dancing," she said.

"I don't care if you don't."

"Or maybe we should wait until the actual dance starts, later on."

"It's a deal," I said quickly.

"Deal."

"What's your name?" I asked.

The band kicked into another song, and I could barely make out what she said.

"Did you say Trixie?" I asked, repeating what I'd heard.

She flashed that amazing smile again and nodded.

Just then, Sherri Mitchell marched up and began speaking directly to Trixie. I couldn't make out what they were saying, but neither looked happy.

"Young man, the dessert station will be ready after dinner," Sherri Mitchell said clearly over the din of the youth band. "This young lady is needed in the kitchen." She pointed to a curtained off area in the back corner of the gym. "Please take a seat and enjoy your meal while our worship team plays for you. Be sure to reflect on the words."

It was then I realized that the band had switched from playing laid back twangy surf music and was now singing a song about Jesus. But even more importantly, Trixie was being led away from me, and into the kitchen.

I understood. She was a good girl and I was a piece of shit jailbird. If I was a church dance chaperone, I'd steer her away from a guy like me too, but I had to talk to her again before the night was over. I walked back to the table feeling simultaneously like I was floating and had been gut punched.

"What the hell, bro?" Screek asked as I sat down. "What's up with the disappearing act. I thought you came here to chow down. You'd better hurry before dinner time is over."

I pushed my plate away. "It's okay. I'm not really that

hungry anymore."

"Have you lost your mind?" Screek asked mid-bite of his burger.

"I was just over there talking to this girl, Trixie."

"I noticed. Looks like the pastor's wife noticed too."

"I've gotta talk to her again, man. She's fucking perfect."

"She's pretty hot, for sure."

"No. She's perfect." I flopped back in the metal chair. "Funny, smart, beautiful…"

"No girl is perfect, bro."

"Joe Versus the Volcano is her favorite movie," I replied.

"No fucking way."

I nodded. Having just proved my point, Screek went back to his food, leaving me to my thoughts, which consumed me for the rest of the night.

TWO

BURNING SAINTS

Spike

THE BAND PLAYED for another half hour or so. It was hard to tell, as every song sounded pretty much like the last one and they all used words I didn't quite understand like 'sanctified' and 'redeemed.' Plus, I never knew if they were supposed to be singing for us, to God, to Jesus or to some chick named Hosannah. I was relieved when they stopped playing, but only briefly, because after the music came the preaching.

I had become a guest of the Lakewood Youth Correctional Center two days after my fourteenth birthday and over the past four years, I'd heard a thousand sermons delivered by a hundred different preachers. Some talked about love and forgiveness, others about heaven and hell, but it always boiled down to believing in something that I couldn't see. Therefore, the very notion of God was a hard no from me, but I knew how to smile and nod enough during a sermon to keep the attention off of me.

As a young child, I'd learned the skill of looking like I was paying attention while letting my mind go to a completely different place. A skill I was currently trying but failing to employ. All I could think about was Trixie and when I'd get to talk to her again. By the time the preacher was delivering the obligatory altar call I was crawling out of my skin. When he asked us all to close our eyes and bow our heads, I made a break for the kitchen. I knew from experience that every preacher would begin his prayer with his eyes closed but would ultimately open them to count the hands of those who wanted to be 'saved from eternal damnation.' I had a very brief window of time, and I wasn't about to waste it.

I stayed low, moving as quickly as I could in the sand. As difficult as it was to walk in, I was thankful for its sound deadening properties. I stayed hidden in the shadows, finally making my way to the makeshift kitchen. I slowly poked my head through the thick black curtain to find Sherri Mitchell standing, arms folded and high-heel-shoed foot tapping on the vinyl flooring. With her bottle dyed red hair, and pearl necklace, all she needed was rolling pin to complete the look of a nineteen fifty's housewife waiting at home for her drunken husband to walk through the door.

* * *

Trixie

"What exactly do you think you're doing?" my mother

screeched at a startled Spike, interrupting Pastor Marty's prayer.

"I...I'm sorry, I was just looking for the... men's room," he said with a smile, his head, still the only thing poking through the makeshift pipe and drape wall.

Spike's smile was the most adorable thing I'd ever seen in my life. It was a crooked sort of grin that pulled up and to the right. Too me it felt like a window into a sweet soul, wrapped in an otherwise tough exterior.

"Get in here, right now," my mother ordered, and Spike complied.

"I apologize, ma'am, I—"

"The restrooms are through the double doors and down the hall, but I believe you knew that already." She narrowed her eyes and gave him her signature death glare. "Didn't you?"

"Yes, ma'am. I didn't mean to cause any trouble. Really, I was, just—"

"Sneaking in here to bother my—"

"What the hell is going on in here?" a man in a blue and grey uniform asked, barging into the kitchen.

"I caught one of your inma...*boys* sneaking into the kitchen in order to fraternize with one of our students."

"Kane," the man said, staring daggers at Spike. "You'd better have a good reason for being in this kitchen."

"I asked him to come," I rushed to say. "It's all my fault. Spike didn't do anything wrong."

Spike looked at me as if I were a puzzle to be worked out.

"What are you talking about?" my mother asked. "Why on earth would you ask *this* boy to come back here?"

The way she said this made my flesh crawl. As Christians, we were commanded by Jesus to show only mercy and compassion to everyone around us, and yet she was the most judgmental person I'd ever known. And having grown up in the church my entire life, that was truly saying something.

"Spike and I were talking earlier as I was setting up the dessert stand, and he asked if he could help with anything," I lied.

"Yes?" my mother pressed.

"I said, no thank you, but come by the kitchen after dinner because we could always use an extra hand washing the dishes once the tables are cleared."

"Is that right, Kane?" the uniformed man asked. "You'd better not lie to me, or I'll know."

"I was just coming by to help, that's all. Just like she said," Spike said, smiling at me.

He looked like a movie star who'd stepped off the screen, walked out of the theater, and straight into this gym. I'd never seen or met anyone like him, and yet, I felt compelled to lie to my mother to protect him.

"If these good people need help, I'll assign it. Now, get back to your table and I'll deal with you later."

"That won't be necessary, Sergeant," my mother said, snapping back into her sweet, submissive voice. "We're here to serve you and your boys tonight. Please, back to your seats now, and we'll forget about this whole mix up, okay?"

"Of course." The sergeant nodded. "My apologies for the interruption."

"Sorry, everyone," Spike said, addressing everyone in the kitchen, but lingering on me, before exiting.

As soon as Spike and the Sergeant were gone, my mother spun me around to face her, whispering to me through clenched teeth made to look like a smile from a distance, "You are not to speak with that boy or any other one of these little criminals again. Do I make myself perfectly clear, young lady?"

I forced myself not to glare at her. "I thought the whole point of this dance was to be an example of Jesus's service and mercy."

"You can do that from inside here."

"But, what about the dance? I worked so hard on it with my friends. Can't I at least spend time with them tonight?"

"This isn't about us, remember. It's about serving Jesus, just like you said. That should be all the reward you need. Don't let me catch you outside of this area tonight. I'll let you know when Kenneth is ready to drive us home. In the meantime, you're on dishes and I suggest you spend some serious time in prayer while you're doing them."

I wondered if prayer included an imaginary voodoo doll in the shape of my mother I was metaphorically sticking pins into.

* * *

Spike

Once out of the kitchen, Hopper pulled me aside, yanking me up by my collar. "The only reason I don't ship your ass back to Lakewood is because until now you've been an okay kid the whole time I've been assigned to the House. You don't talk back, and you always come up clean during shakedowns, but if I find out that girl was lying to cover for you, I will personally make sure the warden tacks on another six months, and you'll serve it in gen pop. You got that?"

"Yes, sir."

"Find a chair. Sit in it. Stay in it." He released me. "Dismissed."

I planted myself down where I had eyes on both the

dance floor and the kitchen. Once the dance started, Hopper couldn't possibly keep his eyes on me all night. He'd eventually have to break up a fight, warn someone about dancing too close, or take a leak. Whatever it was, the second his eyes were off me, I was gonna make a beeline for Trixie. I didn't have a phone number or address to give her, so I was gonna ask her to meet me at Eastport Plaza on the Saturday after my release, but she was nowhere to be seen for the rest of the night. She was gone and I had no way of getting a hold of her. I was a sad sack the entire bus ride home.

"Cheer up, man," Screek said, giving me a gentle elbow. "A month from now you'll be a free man, surrounded by young, available women."

I glared at him.

"I'm just saying. By then you'll have forgotten all about that chick."

I shook my head. "She was perfect. I'm telling you."

"Or...you haven't been that close to a hot chick in years, and 'Little Spike' is doing all the thinking right now."

"You don't get it," I grumbled.

"I'll accept your humble apology a month from now, when you're laying ass deep in a pile of beauties."

"Why exactly does my release look like a hip hop video to you?" I cocked my head. "Once I'm out, I'll have no place to live, no job, and no money. What about all that screams 'chick magnet' to you?"

"You know my theory," Screek replied.

I rolled my eyes. "Oh, shit. Not this again."

"A man has a solid shot with any woman he desires as long as he meets two criteria. Come on, ol' Spikey boy... say them with me."

"He's confident," I grumbled.

"Aaaand..."

"And at least fifty percent less of a douchebag than her last boyfriend."

Screek wiped away a mock tear. "I know I'm not supposed to say things like this, but you're my favorite student."

"What if I can't find her once I get out?"

"Are you fucking kidding me?"

"Keep it down, Dawson, or we'll all ride back in silence," Hopper barked.

"Yes, sir," he replied before turning back to me. "Seriously, bro?" Screek whisper shouted. "I thought you'd been listening to me."

"According to your theory, I could have any woman in the world, is that right?" I challenged.

"So long as the aforementioned two criteria are met, yes."

"Well, I want Trixie."

"My release date is only three weeks after yours," he murmured.

"What's that got to do with anything?"

"Because I plan on plowing through as much pussy as humanly possible once I'm out of here, and that's gonna be a lot harder without my wingman by my side."

"I won't leave you hanging."

"If you're hung up on some chick, you will."

"Plowing pussy. Getting hung up on chicks? Who the fuck are we, the T-birds?" I grumbled.

"Look, my point is, there are tons of interesting, beautiful young women in the greater Portland area. Perhaps we should meet more than a few of them before you start writing your wedding vows."

"Do whatever you want," I replied. "But I'm telling you, by the time you get out, Trixie and I will be together."

Screek shook his head. "Where did I go wrong?"

"I promise I'll still be your wingman. I won't let you down."

He shrugged. "Well, at least your mystery date has a unique name. I mean, how many Trixies can there be in Portland?"

What neither of us realized was that it would, in fact, be impossible to find her.

THREE

BURNING SAINTS

Spike

Present day...

"**E**ASY, EASY, EASY!" Ropes shouted as I lowered the chassis. "Not so fast, you'll scratch the chrome."

"I've got it," I replied.

"Don't let it tilt or the frame will warp."

I paused. "Do *you* wanna do it?"

"No, you're better with the forklift than me," he replied.

I cocked my head. "Then how about you let me do my

job?"

"Sorry, man. I've been working on the wiring for three weeks and had to try five different motors before I found the right one. If anything happens to the chassis before I can assemble this beauty and sell her, I'll be forced to drown you in the Willamette."

"If you're gonna drown me in a river, could you at least make it the Columbia? It's cleaner and more... majestic."

"Tell ya what. Make it down from there safely and I'll gladly let you choose the body of water where your eventual homicide will take place."

"You *do* know the magic words," I said, as I deftly maneuvered my payload down from high storage to the ground.

"See. Not a scratch," I said.

Ropes tussled my hair. "That's my boy."

My biological father was a nomad biker my mother shacked up with from time to time before, and a little while after, I was born. He didn't put his name on my birth certificate, and he didn't stick around long enough for the ink to have dried even if he had. Growing up, my mother instilled in me the value of not harboring any bitterness for the man. She told me straight up that some people aren't up to the task of parenting, and that we were better off not having a man like that around. Even as a little kid that logic made sense to me. It didn't stop me from wishing I had a dad around, but I learned to make do with whatever father figure happened to come into my life.

At the top of my list of role models was Ropes. He served as a combination father figure and older brother. He was the one who picked me up from the House on the day of my release, and I'd been under his tutelage and protection ever since. He taught me about bikes, about club life, and what it means to be a brother. He was not only my teacher, mentor, and the one who sponsored me for membership, but Ropes was the only other guy in the club who loved to read as much as I did. As such, we could talk endlessly about nearly any subject, and often would, to the dismay of our brothers.

Ropes gave me a thumbs up. "Park that thing and help me with final assembly, will ya? The buyer is coming to pick her up tomorrow morning and I need to make sure everything is tip top."

"I'd love to, but I can't. I've got some work I've gotta do."

"You tell diet Thor, that whatever it is he needs you to do can wait an hour or two."

"Not Sweet Pea's orders," I replied.

"Well, unless you're doing something for Minus, tell whoever it is to fuck off and find someone else so you can help me."

"You sure about that?"

"Hell, yes," Ropes said emphatically.

"Okay, gimmie a sec. I just need to text Devlin and tell her you said for her to fuck off and…what was it? I want to make sure I get the wording exactly how you said it."

"You text her one single solitary character and death by tributary will be too good for you."

I slid my phone back into my pocket.

He cocked his head. "What's my wife got you doing for her, now?"

"You know those shelves me and Tacky built for her last week?"

"Lemme guess. Time to stock them?"

I smiled. "It's almost like you know her."

"Doesn't she have employees for that kind of shit?"

"Not according to her," I replied. "Devlin told me she

doesn't have employees. She merely provides a kick ass workspace for top artists to work. She takes a flat cut and artists may come and go as they please."

"What she needs is a shop manager and I keep telling her that. Someone to handle inventory and stupid shit like building shelves."

"I don't mind helping her out. Besides, she's gonna do a back piece for me once I get some time off."

Ropes chuckled. "I don't recall you *ever* taking a day off. You're like a goddamned great white shark. If you stop swimming, you'll sink right down to the bottom of the ocean."

"Either way, it doesn't matter. I haven't figured out exactly what I want, so until I do that, I'm gonna 'bank' as many work hours as possible."

Tacky pulled up to the warehouse and parked his bike, practically jumping off as he did.

"Is she ready to play?" he asked, excitedly.

Ropes shook his head.

He frowned. "Isn't the buyer coming tomorrow?"

"Yeah, but since the two of you pussies seem to do whatever my wife tells you to do, I'm barely going to finish final assembly before he arrives."

"Shit, man. I was hoping to get some playing time in before she was gone."

"Me, too," Ropes replied. "I always like to know if there are any bugs that need to be worked out before the sale but working on my own doesn't leave much time for play."

"Would the two of you please stop griping," I said. "It's not going to take us all day to stock some shelves. We'll be back in a couple of hours. In time to help you with the machine and get some serious play time in so I can kick both your asses."

"Kick my ass?" Ropes asked, incredulously. "Sonny,

I was playing this machine when you were still shitting in your pants."

"You've been playing it since last year?" Tacky asked.

"You know what I hear in both your voices?" I asked. "Fear. That's what I hear."

Ropes had been an avid player, collector, and restorer of vintage pinball machines for most of his life. A passion he passed onto me and Tacky, a brother I'd recruited and patched in with. His current deal involved a 1979 Gorgar machine from Williams, widely known as the first synthesized talking pinball machine. When Ropes bought it, the chassis was mangled and twisted, but I got it looking like it came straight off the factory floor.

Of course, club life wasn't all pinball and tattoo shops. It was about brotherhood, being with a crew that has your back, and about riding, which was one of the only ways I could lose myself for a while. Learning to ride saved my life, redirected my purpose, and set me firmly on the path I'm on today.

Looking back on it now, it's amazing how close I came to never knowing Ropes or the Burning Saints MC at all.

* * *

Eight years ago...

"Inmate 5014429. Kane, Jesse?" the desk sergeant asked.

"Yes, ma'am," I replied, rising to my feet.

"Please step forward to the yellow line."

I did as I was asked, acutely aware that in a few short moments, I wouldn't have to take orders from anyone anymore. Even though I'd spent the last chunk of my sentence at the House, I still had to be 'processed out' at

Lakewood. I was strip-searched to make sure I wasn't smuggling out notes or contraband for my fellow inmates. I'd only been back to Lakewood a few times since moving into the House, while helping Hopper or Fieldy, but I hadn't been back inside until now. Being back in processing brought into focus how long I'd been here, and the time that had needlessly been taken from me. I rarely gave myself the luxury of such thoughts, but now that freedom was literally outside two sets of security doors, they were beginning to seep in.

"The processing for your release is now complete. Please sign here for your personal effects, which you may pick up on the silver table once I've released you."

I scribbled out my signature and she spoke the words I'd been waiting to hear for four years, two months, and twelve days.

"Mr. Kane. You are free to go. Sergeant Hopper will escort you out. Have a good day, a good life, and please don't come back."

"No, ma'am, I don't intend to."

Hopper and I walked outside where he addressed me one last time, "Look, Kane. I think you're a good kid who managed to step into a pile of real deep shit. Don't let this bad start to your young life define who you are. Do you understand what I'm sayin' to ya?"

"Yes, sir. I do."

"Do something good with your life. Show those rich assholes who railroaded you that they were wrong. And don't let those bastards try to grind you down again."

"Thank you, sir. I appreciate it."

"Someone coming to pick you up?" He asked, looking around.

"No, but there was an envelope with three dollars in quarters for the payphones outside in my release packet. I've got friends in the area that I can call."

"Alright, then," Hopper said, patting my shoulder, "Good luck to you, Spike."

And then I was alone. For the first time in over four years, I was alone, and it felt amazing... for about seventeen seconds, then came panic, mixed with fear and dread. I'd lied to Hopper. I knew absolutely no one in this area. In fact, I knew absolutely no one in any area. I had no family, no friends, no money, no job, no place to stay, and no way to get there if I did.

I started going through my mental list of options of how to obtain money, food, and lodging.

1. Man Whore – Qualifications: I'm young, fresh outta prison fit, and swing a decent meat hammer. Pros: Get paid to fuck rich desperate housewives. Cons: You'll actually be giving blowjobs in the Portland airport bathrooms. Verdict: Best to pass and leave that position open for someone with a true passion for it.
2. Life Coach - Qualifications: None, but that hasn't seemed to stop anyone else in the past from becoming one. Pros: Get paid to fuck rich desperate housewives. Cons: I'd have to wear a man bun and sign up for Twitter. Verdict: Hard Pass
3. Barista – this just feels like I'm saying life coach again, so I'll skip to number—

Before I could think of the next possible career path, my thoughts were interrupted by the roar of exhaust pipes. I turned to see a primo black and orange Plymouth Road Runner Superbird pull up to the curb in front of me. The driver got out. "You Kane?"

I gave him a chin lift. "Who's asking?"

"My name's Ropes and I've been sent here to pick up a kid named Jesse Kane."

"Sent by who?"

"The President of my club, the Burning Saints. A man named Cutter."

I shook my head. "Don't know anyone by that name."

"Yeah, well he knows you. Knows your dad, at least."

"Bullshit," I said.

"Your old man is Kodiak, a nomad who used to ride with the Apex Predators way back in the day."

"I wouldn't know. I've never met him."

"Your mom never mentioned him?"

"Don't fucking talk about my mother," I said, throwing my shit down and moving towards him. "I don't fucking know you, man, so don't say shit about my mother."

Ropes put his hands in the air and turned his head to the side. A sign of respectful submission. "No disrespect to you or your family."

"What the fuck are you doing here?"

Ropes put his hands down slowly. "When your father got word of your mother's passing, he reached out to Cutter and asked him to keep an eye on you once you were released. Today is that day, so I'm here to pick you up and drive you to Portland so Cutter can make good on his promise."

"No thanks."

"What do you mean, no thanks?"

"It's pretty fucking self-explanatory. I don't know you, and I'm not just gonna jump into your cool car just because you say you know a guy who knows my sperm donor. You may as well be driving a panel van that says free candy on it, you fucking perv."

Ropes laughed. "Okay kid, since you've clearly got better options, I'll take off and leave you to explore them. But if you change your mind, there's a shit ton of take-out food, clean clothes, and your own private room at the Tall Pines Motel, about two miles up the road. Room 117. You can pick up your key at the front desk. I'll be next door in 119, drinking imported beer, if you need me. I'll be wheels up by eight o' clock sharp tomorrow morning.

With that, he hopped back into the Plymouth and peeled off, leaving me once again alone with my thoughts.

I stood there for about three minutes before I hoofed in the direction he'd indicated, relieved to find a key waiting for me just as he said.

I could confidently eliminate man-whore as one of my options of survival. Now I just had to figure out what this club wanted, and maybe I could forget about slinging coffee or advice.

FOUR

BURNING SAINTS

Trixie

"**I**'M TAKING A stand," I said to my best friend, Gemma. It was nine o'clock Saturday night, and I had her on speaker as I got ready for bed.

"Really?" she droned sarcastically.

"Yes, really. I'm a grown woman, I shouldn't have to go to church *every* Sunday."

"Hmm-mmm."

"I'm serious this time, Gem. I'm going to be honest with my mom." I spread night cream on my face and stared at myself in the mirror.

"You're not going to be honest with your mum and

you know it," she countered. Gemma was British but she'd been living in the States since sixth grade and although she'd kept her accent, she hadn't held onto her politeness. She was brutally honest and I loved her for it.

I sighed. "No, you're right, I probably won't be completely honest. I mean, how do you tell your uber religious mother you don't really believe everything she believes anymore? It will destroy her."

"It won't destroy her. Your brother coming out didn't destroy her, so you saying you don't believe in the magic man in the sky probably won't even be on her radar."

She had a point. "You know boys and their mothers. She's always loved them more."

"Well, that makes her a bitch," she said. Gemma hated my parents. I mean, I didn't blame her, they'd always said she was a bad influence on me, and highly objected to my ten-plus year friendship with her.

"Does that make her a bitch?"

"Yes," she hissed. "She's awful to you and you just sit there and take it. You don't deserve to be treated that way. Plus, you're the good one. Your brothers went off the rails years ago… your dad's words, not mine. I happen to love your brothers."

"I do too. And he only said that because Matty brought a boy home for dinner and kissed him in front of everyone. They were shocked."

This had been his first year of college and it was how he came out to my parents. I was just starting high school and my parents were convinced my precious, virgin ears should not have heard any of his declaration, but Jenson and I had always known Mattias was gay, and we didn't give one shit about it. He was our brother, and love is love, but my parents were, and still are, concerned he's damned to hell because of his 'lifestyle.' That lifestyle being him in a committed relationship with his partner for

31

the past six years (not the boyfriend he'd brought home initially, to be clear). There were, like, twelve before Ronnie because, let's be honest, both my brothers were, ah, shall we say, very lovable?

"Well, they could have kept their opinions to themselves and talked about it alone instead of kicking your brother and his boyfriend out of their house," Gemma continued.

"That is very true," I agreed.

"And don't even get me started on Jenson. That man is divine."

Jenson was the middle kid and worked at a local tattoo shop in Portland.

"You need to put your labia back in your panties, Gem."

"I'll do no such thing if it means I get to suck your brother's d—"

"La, la, la, la," I sang, then made barfing noises. "Gross."

"You need to move out."

"I can't afford to move out," I said. "I need to find a better paying job—"

"And one without a creep named Dan."

I shuddered. "Preferably without anyone creepy."

I was a receptionist at a law firm and worked with an attorney who was an absolute perv and made the most inappropriate comments, including, but not limited to, "How many men did you take home this weekend?" and "I bet you clean up at the bars on the weekend, sweetheart." It had gotten so bad, I was forced to make a formal complaint to H.R. this past week. They'd promised to take care of it, but I wasn't overly confident anything would be done, considering he was a founding partner.

Gemma chuckled. "Want to get brunch tomorrow, you know, since you're not going to church?"

"Yes. But let me just tell Mom first then we can confirm brunch."

"Hmm mm."

"I'm going to do it. I really am," I avowed.

"I'll believe it when I see it."

I wrinkled my nose. We'd been here before, more times than I'd like to count, so her not believing me was fair.

"I'll text you when it's done."

"Can't wait," she breathed out.

"Wish me luck."

"You don't need luck, you need balls."

"Well, wish me balls then."

Gemma laughed. "Okay, sister from another mister, good balls."

"Ugh, now I keep thinking about those truck balls. So tacky."

"Agreed. Okay, I'm going to let you go so you can do the thing."

"Right. Okay. Talk to you tomorrow."

"Bye, love."

We hung up and I sat on the edge of my bed, trying to figure out how to tell my mother I was not going to go to church with her the next day.

* * *

"So, what did you tell her?" Gemma asked, sipping her second mimosa.

I grimaced.

"You didn't tell her."

"I told her I would not be attending church this morning," I replied.

"Mmm hmm," she replied, sounding unconvinced. "And did you tell her why?"

33

"I told her I was sick," I admitted. "Too sick to join her today."

Gemma gasped. "Christine Esther Mitchell, you *lied* to your mother?"

"I did." I bit my lip. "I'm going to hell."

"I don't know about hell, but you're at least gonna do some hard time at the DMV."

I groaned.

"Did you lie to her face or over text?"

I dropped my eyes to the table. "Text."

I lived in the converted apartment above my parents' garage. It was somewhat of a compromise they made to give me a little bit of freedom, and besides, with school, I couldn't afford rent in Portland, so now that I'd been working and saving for a little while, I hoped to move fully out within the year.

Gemma nodded to my glass. "Drink more and you won't care."

I chuckled, finishing off my *first* mimosa.

"You know, your brother's working at a new shop that's not far from here," Gemma said, casually.

"I did *not* know that. How do you?"

She grinned her evilest grin. "I stalk his Zippypics account."

"When will your gross obsession with my brother end?"

"When we're married with three kids and five dogs and live in a bed and breakfast inside a basic cable Christmas movie, where I cook pancakes in an all-white kitchen while he rams me proper hard from behind."

"Oh my word, you're insane. Jens isn't ready to settle down. I don't know if he ever will be."

Gemma shrugged. "I still think we should go see him after brunch."

"You think we should see Jenson *every* day."

She rolled her eyes. "Not every day, but we're right down the road from the shop, so let's go. Maybe I'll get another tattoo."

"If you want Jens, you'll need to plan a few months ahead," I reminded her.

"Well, then, we can check out the shop and I'll make an appointment."

I smiled. "Okay, we'll go. Just no pictures and I need to be back before their lunch is over. If Mom and Dad find out I lied, I…"

"You'll what?" Gemma challenged. "Die? Get smoted? What?"

"Smoted isn't a word."

"Well, it should be."

I laughed. "Yes, yes, it should."

Our server arrived and set the bill on the table which Gemma snatched right up.

"Hey," I ground out. "It's my turn to pay."

"Oops, too slow." She handed her credit card to the man and he walked away.

What a lot of people didn't know was that Gemma had money. Like, gazillions. At twenty-three, she was one of the youngest multi-millionaires in the world, having held the title since she was eighteen. Trust fund baby, and an honest to goodness 'lady' to boot.

Once the bill was paid, we headed down Mississippi toward Jenson's shop. Since we were barely a block away, we walked.

* * *

Spike

I parked the van right out front of Devlin's shop, and carefully exited onto the narrow street. It was a beautiful fall day, and the popular neighborhood was alive with cyclists, dog walkers, and strolling couples, sipping from recyclable coffee cups from one of the myriads of local coffee shops. Tacky rode his bike ahead of me and was already busy working inside.

I opened the back door of the panel van, grabbed a hand truck, and set it on the curb. I closed and locked the van, and stepped onto the sidewalk, stopping dead in my tracks before I made it any further.

About ten yards away, and walking right toward me, was Trixie. *The* Trixie. *My* Trixie. The girl that I'd fantasized about so much, I wasn't entirely sure I hadn't made her up. The girl, who, for almost a decade, only existed in my mind and on the pages of my journal, was currently walking down Mississippi Avenue. Adding to my state of shock, was the fact that she stopped at Devlin's shop, opening the door for whoever she was with.

Before I had the chance to come to my senses I blurted out, "Trixie," but she didn't seem to notice. I abandoned the hand truck and walked toward her, calling out once again, "Trixie." This time she turned around and looked at me with a puzzled expression.

"Who's Trixie?" the woman with her asked, and Trixie's look of confusion turned to one of recognition.

"Spike?"

The sound of her voice saying my name almost sent me to the concrete.

"I...I can't believe it's you," I stammered.

"Oh, my gosh," she said, her gloved hands going to her mouth. "You were at the Beach Blanket Blowout dance."

I grinned. "Yeah, that...that was me."

"I can't believe you remembered me." Trixie seemed as shocked as I was.

"I couldn't possibly forget," I replied.

"How did you even recognize me? That was five or six years ago, wasn't it?"

"Eight years, actually, and you look exactly the same," I said, making her blush exactly like I did the first time we met.

"I hate to break this to you, but you may need to start wearing glasses." She squinted at me. "My uncle is an optometrist if you need a recommendation."

I locked eyes with her. "I see just fine."

Trixie's friend cleared her throat. "Would you like to introduce me to your fit as fuck friend?"

"Oh, my gosh, I'm sorry." Trixie turned to her friend. "Gemma, this is Spike. Spike, this is my best friend, Gemma."

"It's nice to meet you," I said, shaking Gemma's hand.

"Spike and I met at a dance at our church just before we graduated high school."

"Well, Trixie was graduating, but I was to be nearly released from prison," I corrected her.

"Triiiixie," Gemma sang out in her heavy British accent. "How bloody adorable is that?"

"Why is that 'bloody adorable'?" I asked, confused by Gemma's reaction.

"My name isn't Trixie. It's actually Chrissy," she said.

I cocked my head. "What's going on?"

Trixie blushed. "At the dance, when you asked for my name, you must have misheard me."

"What are you talking about? After you said your name, I confirmed that you said Trixie."

She bit her lip. "I thought it was cute and I didn't want to correct you."

"Cute? It's so fucking sweet I have a cavity." Gemma made a motion to pick her teeth as she made gagging noises.

"Besides," Trixie shrugged. "I never thought I'd see

37

you after that night, so I didn't think it'd make a difference."

"Well, it certainly explains why I could never find you," I said.

"Find me? You seriously looked for me after that night?"

"Of course, I did. I wanted to talk to you more, but Sergeant Hopper and that ginger bitch from your church kept us separated."

A deep laugh leapt from Gemma's mouth. "Ginger bitch is right."

"That was my mom," Trixie said.

"Oh, shit. I'm sorry," I rushed to say before adding, "In my mind, she's kind of been a villain in the story of that night."

"She's the villain of *every* story," Gemma grumbled.

"She's not that bad," Trixie countered.

Gemma raised an eyebrow. "Uh, yeah, she is. You're just still stuck in her brainwashing vortex." Her friend focused on me. "At some point she's gonna figure it out, it's just taking longer than I'd like for her to get away from these psychos."

"Gemma!" Trixie squeaked. "Don't be mean."

"Being honest isn't being mean, love. You need to remember that."

"*Anyway.*" Trixie rolled her eyes and took a deep breath, fixing a smile to her beautiful face. She had the cutest fuckin' dimple in her right cheek and even if her smile might be a little forced, it still transformed her face. "I can't believe you remembered me, or that night, honestly. It was chaos."

"You remembered me," I pointed out.

"Yeah, but that's different."

"How's it different?"

"You weren't like any guy I'd ever met before in my

life. You seemed more full of life than anyone at our church, but also so lost and sad. I prayed for you for a long time."

"You prayed for *me*?"

She smiled and nodded.

"Well, here we are." I cocked my head. "Maybe there *is* a god after all."

Gemma let out a snort. "Highly doubtful."

"Gemma, shut it," Trixie hissed.

Before I could ask her anything else, Devlin walked out of the shop. "There you are. I thought you might have been beamed up or something. I saw you pull up, then, poof, you disappeared."

"Yeah, sorry, sweetheart, just met an old friend." I smiled. "Trix—I mean, Chrissy, this is Devlin. And this is Gemma."

Chrissy shook Devlin's hand. "I'm Jenson's sister."

"Oh my god, seriously?" Devlin pulled her in for a hug as she glared at me. "Why the hell didn't you say that first?"

"I didn't know," I admitted.

Chrissy chuckled. "We didn't get that far."

"Well, come on inside," Devlin ordered, then focused on me. "And you have work to do."

I frowned. "Yeah, got it. Don't leave before touching base, Chrissy, yeah?"

"Oh, please don't call me Chrissy," she begged. "I like the other name better."

I grinned. "Okay, Trixie. Don't leave before we touch base."

"I can do that."

I nodded, then headed back outside to grab my hand truck.

FIVE

BURNING SAINTS

Trixie

"**B**ITCH," GEMMA HISSED as we followed Devlin into the shop. "You have some serious explaining to do."

I rolled my eyes. "There's nothing to explain. You basically heard everything on the street."

"That's not what I mean, and you know it."

"I don't know it."

"That man is hot as fuck and it's totally obvious he wants into your knickers. It's obvious he wanted into your knickers back in the day as well. Why the hell didn't you tell me about hottie convict, biker boy back then?"

I closed my eyes briefly.

"Chris."

I face her. "What?"

"Why didn't you tell me about him?" she pressed. "You tell me everything. Even back then."

"Because he was mine," I hiss-pered.

Her eyes widened and then she smiled gently. "You really liked him."

I nodded.

"Is that why you've kicked every guy to the curb before the first date flowers had a chance to wilt?"

"Can we not talk about this right now?"

"Sissy?" my brother's voice called out.

"Sure, love. But we *are* going to revisit it."

I turned back toward the red velvet curtain to see my brother emerging from it with a concerned look on his face. "What's wrong?"

"What?" I cocked my head. "Nothing. Can't a sister just come and see her brother in his place of business?"

His eyes glanced behind me and he smirked before pulling me in for a hug. "You had something to do with this, Gem, didn't you?"

I chuckled. "She did not. I'm sure you're busy, so we won't keep you. We just wanted to say hi."

"I've got twenty minutes before my next client. I've got time." He released me and held the curtain back so we could precede him to the back.

"Oh my word," I breathed out as I took in the space. Stations that looked a bit like a hair salon, only way cooler, were set up with men and women already in chairs getting their tattoos. I noticed that every single area had privacy curtains that could be closed, but at the moment they were all open. "This is so cool."

"Yeah," Jenson agreed. "Devlin runs a tight ship."

"Show me your book," I demanded.

He chuckled.

"You can't deny me now," I pointed out. "If you show potential clients your art, you *have* to show your sister."

Jenson had *always* drawn. Always. He'd doodle in church, he'd doodle in school, but his 'real' art, the stuff of his heart was hidden away in his room, usually some place I couldn't find it (I'd tried) and he'd always refused to show me because he said it was personal.

He handed me an iPad which contained scans of his work. I squealed and started to swipe through drawings. I gasped when I came upon a pencil drawn sketch of me. "When did you draw this?"

"Ah…" He leaned down and pointed to the date. "You were in high school I think."

I squinted, focusing on the fading date and bit my lip. "That's the day after the Beach Blanket Blowout dance. Why do I look so sad?"

"Because you were," Jenson said. "You locked yourself in your room and cried. Well, after you yelled at Mom for an hour because she'd been a mega bitch for something."

I met his eyes. "I never called her a bitch."

He grinned. "No. I'm paraphrasing. But remember? Matty and I snuck into your room and brought you gummy worms because you were grounded. You never did tell us why you were so upset. Not even Matt, which was weird because you tell him everything."

"I know why," Gemma said.

"Shut it," I warned, then continued to 'flip' through his 'book.' "These are amazing, Jens. I don't know why you'd hide any of this from us. Seriously. It's unbelievable."

"Thanks, sissy. I appreciate that."

Gemma flopped down in one of his chairs just as Spike sauntered over. It took everything in me not to let out a schoolgirl sigh.

"Hey." He gave my brother a chin lift. "I'm Spike."

"Jenson." My brother shook his hand.

"Dev said you had a book I could look at."

Jenson grinned. "Oh, yeah, man. You lookin' at getting more ink?"

Spike nodded, his eyes going to me.

"I'll scroll back." I flipped Jenson's 'book' back to the beginning and handed Spike the iPad. Gemma rummaged through her purse to grab her phone while Jenson pulled his from his pocket and I watched Spike go through the sketches.

He swiped through, studying the pictures while simultaneously glancing at me over the screen. "Fuck, man, these are unreal. Devlin's word didn't do you justice."

"Right," I said excitedly. "Isn't he amazing?"

"Yeah, Trixie, he's amazing."

Jenson's head whipped up. "Trixie?"

"Just drop it, Jens," I warned.

Spike gave me a wink.

I bit the inside of my cheek and forced my face to stay neutral. Oh my word, the man just winked at me and I swear my panties might have just flooded. I was going to have to pray a little harder tonight. Very quietly. Actually, silently in case my voice carried on the wind and my mother heard it.

* * *

Spike

I couldn't stop looking at her. I pretended to be going through her brother's book, but I wasn't really seeing any of the images, I was too busy taking her in.

"See anything you like?" Jenson asked.

I met Trixie's eyes for the umpteenth time and nodded. "Yeah."

She blushed as Jenson bristled. "I meant in the book."

"Jens," she ground out, her tone one of warning. She craned her head toward him and I saw him shrug before she faced me again. "Ignore him."

"It's all good." I chuckled. "Your stuff's good, man. Gonna think about it."

Jenson gave me a chin lift.

"Jenson, your appointment's here," Devlin called.

"We'll leave you to do your thing," Trixie said, hugging her brother.

"Dinner next week, okay?" he asked her. "My treat."

"Sounds perfect."

"I'll walk you out," I offered, half expecting Trixie's big brother to object, but he simply gave me the side eye before I followed the women out to the front of the shop.

The phone was ringing as we passed by the empty desk and it didn't stop for several seconds.

"Is no one around to answer the phones?" Trixie asked.

I shook my head. "Devlin's had a hell of a time getting good help."

Before she could ask another question, the phones started again.

"What's the name of the shop again?" Trixie asked.

"Laughing Crow Ink."

She moved behind the desk and answered the phone. "Laughing Crow Ink, how may I help you? He's with a client right now, can I take a message?" Grabbing a pad of paper beside the phone, she opened a couple of drawers before finding a pen. "And you tried his cell? Oh, okay. No, I'm sorry, I can't give that information out, but I'll be sure to give him the message. Of course. No problem." She hung up and looked our way. "What?"

"Babe, you just answered that phone like you owned the place," Gemma said.

Trixie shrugged. "It's the same phone system I use at work. Plus, the call was for Jens, so I knew exactly where he was. Easy-peasy." She pulled out her phone and sent a text. "Now, the message has been delivered, and we can go."

"Do you need a job?" I asked her.

"Nope, but thanks."

"Did someone grab the phones?" Devlin asked, rushing through the curtains.

"That was me," Trixie said. "Sorry, I didn't mean to overstep. When I hear a phone, my Pavlovian instinct is to make it stop."

Devlin chuckled. "Do you need a job?"

"That's what I asked her," I said.

"No, thank you," Trixie said with a smile. "I've got a great one."

"Well, if that ever changes, will you let me know?" Devlin asked.

"Sure," she said.

"It was great to meet you."

"You too, Devlin."

"Your place is lovely," Gemma added.

"Thanks. We've worked hard to get it here."

"You can say that again," I murmured.

Devlin rolled her eyes. "You have shelves to stock, buddy."

"Be right there," I promised and turned to Trixie as Devlin walked back behind the drapes. "You gonna give me your phone?"

"Why?"

"For your number, love," Gemma said.

"Oh," Trixie squeaked, handing her phone over to me. "Does that mean you're going to call me?"

"Hell, yeah, I am." I added my contact information to her phone, then sent myself a text so I had hers.

"I'll be right outside," Gemma said, smiling at me as she stepped out the front door.

"I can't believe I found you," I said, not wanting her to leave. I was afraid if she walked out the door, I'd never see her again.

"I can't believe you found me, too." Trixie bit her lip and it took everything in me not to throw her up against the reception desk and kiss the fuck out of her. "Please don't disappear on me, okay?"

"Not a chance." I waved my phone in the air. "Got your information now. I'm not letting you go again."

"Promise?" she whispered.

"Fuck, yeah, I promise."

"Can I hug you?"

"Yeah, beautiful, you don't even have to ask." I held my arms out and she wrapped hers around my waist.

"Wow, you smell amazing," she whispered, giving me a squeeze before stepping back. "Sorry, I'm making things awkward."

"Not even close." I smiled. "You sure you have to go?"

"Yes, I need to get home."

"Call me later?"

"Do you want me to call you later?"

"Wouldn't ask if I didn't want."

She smiled. "Well, then, maybe I will."

"Holding you to it, Trixie."

With one last nod, she walked out the door, and I went back to helping Devlin stock the shelves I'd just assembled for her.

* * *

Trixie

I had just closed myself into my little apartment when I heard the garage door open below me. I rushed to take off my makeup and throw my pajamas on, crawling back into

46

bed, just in case my mother were to come looking for me.

Gemma texted asking if I'd made it inside before the warden had caught me, and I'd sent back an eyerolling emoji, but she wasn't far off with how my parents made me feel most days. I needed to make a change, I just didn't know how to do it.

An hour later, there'd been no knock on my door, so I let out a breath of relief, suddenly feeling a little silly I'd worried that my mommy might catch me sneaking back into my home after my salacious brunch with my best friend.

It was ridiculous, really.

I slid out of bed and headed to my kitchen, desperately wanting some tea and maybe a cookie or three. Or maybe I'd try not to eat the cookies. Spike didn't make mention of the fact I'd gained at least forty pounds since high school, and I wore it somewhat well, according to Gemma, but if I had a chance in 'H, E, double hockey sticks' with the sexy biker, I feared gaining any more weight would be a deal breaker for him.

I had just stepped to my sink when I heard, "Christine Esther Mitchell."

I squeaked, spinning to find my mother sitting in my high-backed chair by the window. It was my favorite and one of the few things I'd actually bought on my own.

"Mom! You scared me to death."

She raised an eyebrow. "I thought you were sick."

"I was. I'm feeling much better."

"So sick you went out earlier?"

I blushed, saying nothing in an effort not to lie to her.

"We don't lie to each other in this house, Christine."

I sighed. "I just wanted a break from church, Mama."

"Well, as long as you're living under our roof, you'll go to church every Sunday, honey. That's a deal."

"Technically, I'm living *over* your roof."

"Don't sass me, young lady."

"Please don't talk to me like I'm a little girl."

"Please don't act like a petulant child and I won't have to talk to you like one."

"Look, Mom, I'm sorry I lied about being sick."

"It's not only me you should apologize to," Mom said. "Your father worked very hard on this week's sermon, and perhaps if you'd been there to hear it, you would have a better understanding of the teachings of Jesus and how to better follow them."

"Do you actually think that I haven't heard every sermon possible ten times over by now? The Bible's big, Mama, but it's not that big."

"Christine, what has gotten into you?" Mama demanded. "It's that Gemma girl, isn't it?"

"Mom, Gemma's been my best friend since sixth grade."

"That girl puts wild thoughts into your head and I don't like it."

"How would you know what Gemma and I talk about?" I challenged. "You barely acknowledge she exists as a person, let alone know anything about her. Talk about sermons, I'm sure Daddy has preached more than a few times about the sin of being judgmental."

"That's it, young lady, this impertinence needs to stop right now."

"No, I will pert all I want," I snapped, trying not to laugh at my joke because my mother was obviously taking this inane conversation seriously. "I'm old enough to pert and I've earned the right to pert. In fact, maybe it's not only time to find another place to live, but a different church to attend."

My mother looked like she saw a train barreling toward her and she was tied to the tracks. "Why would you say something so cruel? It would break your father's heart."

"Maybe, for once, this isn't about Daddy. Or you, for that matter. Maybe this time, it's about what I want. What I need."

"Your father is the most anointed teacher of God's word I have ever known. What could you possibly find in another church that you couldn't find at Lifesprings?"

"Maybe it's about what I wouldn't find at another church."

My mother gasped. "What's that supposed to mean?"

"I'd just like to go somewhere where I didn't have a thousand sets of eyeballs pinned on me. Somewhere I'm not a PK and where I don't have to pretend to be perfect all the time."

"Being a pastor's kid doesn't mean being perfect all the time."

"It does to Daddy and it certainly does to you."

"What is that supposed to mean?"

I took a deep breath. "Mom, I feel like I can never do anything right with you. And a lot of the time, I feel like you don't even like me."

"How could you say such a thing? A mother's love for her child is a sacred thing. Something you won't understand until you have children of your own."

"I never said you didn't love me, only that you didn't like me."

"Honestly," she breathed out. "I don't understand where this is coming from."

"It's coming from years of presenting the best version of myself to you in order to gain any amount of true warmth and affection, only to feel like I was coming up short in your eyes. And I don't have to have a child of my own to understand our mother-daughter relationship... or lack thereof."

"We have a perfectly good relationship."

"Do we?" I challenged. "When's the last time the two of us spent any amount of time together?" My mother opened her mouth to say something but I cut her off. "Outside of a church function."

My mother closed her mouth again.

"Exactly," I retorted.

Mom sighed and clasped her hands in her lap.

"Look, Mom, I love you and I'm not saying any of this to make you feel bad. I just need you to see where I'm coming from and honestly, I think I just need space from all of it. The church, this house, you and Daddy. I just want to focus on my job and take some time to figure out who I am outside of Lifesprings and outside of this neighborhood. Good lord, Mama, even the Amish get a Rumspringa."

Mom rolled her eyes, her nose going further up in the air (if that was possible) and she rose to her feet. "I don't know what's brought all this on, and why you're so intent on hurting my feelings, and dishonoring your father, but I hope you're happy while you're out in the world smoking mushrooms and having your Amish orgy." She moved to my door and pulled it open. "Your father and I'll be praying for you."

With that parting shot, she walked out and closed the door behind her.

I bit back tears and grabbed my phone, instinctively scrolling to Gemma's name, only I didn't stop there. I continued to Spike's number and pressed the call button.

He answered on the first ring. "Well, hey there, beautiful."

"Hi."

"What's wrong?"

I burst into tears.

"Fuck. Trixie, honey, what happened?"

Through my hiccups and tears, I filled him in on the

conversation with my mother, my heart no longer breaking, because I was angry. Angry that my mother was making me feel like a pariah when all I'd ever done was try to please her.

"Want me to come get you?" Spike asked.

I bit my lip. "Aren't you busy?"

"Not too busy to come take your mind off something shitty your mom said to you."

"Oh my word, I'd love that," I breathed out.

"You ever been on the back of a bike before?"

"That's a firm no."

He chuckled. "Okay, wear jeans and tall boots. Do you have a leather jacket?"

"Also a firm no. Leather jackets are for strippers and prostitutes."

"Jesus, your mom tell you that?"

"No, actually, that was my dad. One of his sermons."

"Fucking hell," he hissed. "Okay, I've got something that'll work. I've also got an extra helmet. Just dress warm. Where are you?"

"We live in the West Hills."

"Okay, text me the address. I'll be there in about half an hour."

"Okay." I smiled. "Um, Spike?"

"Yeah?"

"Thank you."

"You got it."

He hung up and I made a mad dash back to my bedroom to get ready.

SIX

BURNING SAINTS

Spike

"**I** STILL CAN'T believe you'd never seen that movie before," I said, holding the theater door open for Trixie. I couldn't keep my eyes off of her, and I wondered how long I'd be able to keep my hands off her. I'd spent most of the duration of the movie thinking about, and fighting the urge to, lean over and peel her out of her clothes. Her intoxicating scent permeated the ever-present odor of fifty years of stale popcorn, and it was driving me to distraction.

"What a gentleman," she said, while tugging on the

Red Vine clenched between her teeth, her perfect lips wrapping around the ropes of bright red candy before letting out a quiet laugh. "I almost peed my pants when Large Marge's face went all googly."

"I know your parents were strict, but how could they have deprived you of Pee-wee?" I asked, trying my best to hide how turned on I was by her.

"Are you kidding? I couldn't even watch the Muppets. There was no way Pee-wee was making it onto the approved list."

"The Muppets were forbidden? How is that possible?"

"My mom said Jim Henson was a puppeteer of evil who led a cult of dirty, hippie, felt fetishists, all of whom wanted nothing more than to pollute the minds of young people into a life of smoking dope, and putting their mouths on each other's filthy no-no spots."

I stopped dead in my tracks. "I genuinely have no response to that."

"According to my mother, Satan is hiding around every corner, waiting patiently for the moment I let my guard down."

"Then what?"

Trixie shrugged. "He'll strike, I guess."

"Satan?"

She nodded.

"Satan, as in the devil himself?"

She nodded again.

"Your mom doesn't think Lucifer has more important things to do like drumming up wars, and causing famine, disease, and pestilence? Is she so bold to assume the dark lord has the spare time to lay traps and wait for good, innocent, Christian young women to fall into them?"

Trixie's laugh made me feel better than I had since the first night I met her.

After catching her breath, she said, "I have to ask you a question, but I don't want you to take it the wrong way."

"I'm an open book."

"How is it that a biker who spent most of his youth incarcerated uses words like pestilence and quotes Jean-Paul Sartre?"

"Probably because I *was* incarcerated for most of my youth," I replied. "There's not much to do on the inside but read, play chess with criminals, or play checkers with numbskulls, so I did a lot of reading."

"I'm sorry, Spike, that sounds difficult."

I smiled. "It's okay. Would you like to have coffee and pie with me?"

Trixie's dimpled cheeks flushed, and it took every ounce of my internal strength not to grab her, take her back into one of the empty darkened theaters, and fuck her until tomorrow's matinee.

"I'd love to," she replied.

* * *

Spike

"I know Shari's isn't fancy, but they have killer pie and they're open late," I said as we settled into our booth.

"Are you kidding? What's not to love? Besides, I'm starving. That popcorn was all I've had since brunch with Gemma this morning."

"Welcome to Shari's my name is Beth and I'll be your server tonight." Beth was a haggard sounding woman who looked to be firmly in the back half of a fifty-to-life stretch.

"Well, howdy there Beth," I said, donning a thick but chipper southern drawl. "My name's Spike, juss like it says on m'patch. An' this here is m'new wife Trixie Lou." I motioned to my now blushing bride.

"Howdy," Trixie said, like a true southern belle, completed by a demure, pageant wave and all.

"Can I get the two of you anything to drink while you look over your menus?" Beth asked, unphased by our southern charm.

Trixie motioned for me to order first.

"Coffee for me, please, ma'am," I said.

"Cream or sugar with that?" she asked, without looking up from her notepad.

"Black as molasses if you please."

Trixie nodded in approval. "Mmmmm. But I'll have Splenda and cream, please."

"A pot of coffee coming up," Beth said before pointing to the menu. "Specials are on page two and the pies are on the back. Let me know if you have any questions."

As soon as Beth was out of earshot, Trixie burst into laughter. "Oh my word, my face hurts so bad."

"Nicely done," I said. "It's good to know you wouldn't fold easily under questioning."

She let out a snort. "You have no idea how wrong you are."

"Sometimes you have to spice up the simple moments in life, ya know?"

"Is that what that was all about?"

"Sure. Order coffee as a newly married couple from Texas or take out the trash as a secret agent who's on a deep cover mission. You're going to have to do a million boring things before you die, right? Why not have a little fun while you're doing them?"

"You are definitely the same boy I remember from all those years ago," she said, studying me as if she were an art student and I was a painting on a museum wall.

I closed my menu with a 'thwap,' knowing what I was going to order before we'd even walked in. "Think of how many times she's said that in her life."

"What?"

"*Hi, my name is Beth*...and that whole thing about the specials being on page two...blah, blah, blah. I could never stand to do something so scripted all day long, ya know what I mean?"

"I think I do. Is that why you're a biker? Is it the freedom to do whatever you want that attracts you to that lifestyle?"

"I love how you keep calling me a *biker*. It's cute as fuck," I said, the curse slipping through my stupid lips. "Sorry."

"And I think it's cute as fuck that you keep apologizing to me every time you swear," she whispered, her cheeks glowing red.

"You've never said that word before, have you?"

"Not in public." She bit her lip before sliding her menu up to hide her face as she slumped down into her seat.

Beth came to the table with two official Shari's mugs, a ramekin of individual creamers, and a silver coffee carafe. "You folks figured out what you want to eat?"

"I'll have the Denver omelet, please," Trixie squeaked from behind her menu fort.

"Make that two, would ya," I said, handing my menu to her. "Oh, wait." I paused. "Does a Denver omelet have bell peppers in it?"

"Normally, yes," Beth replied.

"Well, what city makes an omelet that's exactly like a Denver omelet, but without the bell peppers?"

Beth stared at me for a long time. One could say uncomfortably long. It was as if we were gunfighters, and this family friendly chain restaurant was our saloon. Years of waitressing had led to this very moment and Beth was ready.

She was ready fucking spaghetti.

After what felt like an eternity in diner time, the wizened waitress spoke, "I'd have to say Cleveland."

I smiled at her, feeling as satisfied with her answer as I could have possibly been, and replied, "I'll have a Cleveland omelet please, Beth."

I swear I'd fight a rabid bear in a cage match to know exactly what Beth scribbled down on her notepad before turning and heading back to the kitchen. From the look on her face, it could have been anything from 'Denver Om - 86 Peppers,' to the beginnings of her suicide note.

"You can lower yer fences, my darlin'. All is safe on this here ponderosa."

"I swear, I'm going to die, I'm laughing so hard," Trixie gasped from behind her menu. "You have to stop."

"But if'n I stop, she'll know that we're city folks. She's liable to call the sheriff n' round up a posse."

"I'm seriously going to pee, Spike, you need to quit."

I grinned. "Okay, okay, I'll stop."

She took a few deep breaths and wiped her tears away. "Thank you."

I poured Trixie a cup of coffee, adding the cream and sweetener to her specifications, pausing for her to take a drink before I moved on to mine.

"Wow. You hold doors open for women, pour coffee, and placed your napkin on your lap without having to be told. You're quite the gentleman for a biker." She met my eyes. "Actually, you're more of a gentleman than most of the guys I've known."

"There's that 'b' word, again," I teased.

"Okay, if not biker, then what?"

"We usually refer to ourselves as club members, or Saints," I replied.

"Usually?"

I nodded.

"What do you call yourselves other times?"

I smiled. "Bikers."

"I take back what I said about good manners. You seem to have a pathological need to tease women."

"That's not true," I protested. "My need to tease only applies to you."

She blushed. "I'm not used to being teased. My family... well, we don't tease unless it's passive-aggressive digs at one another."

I frowned. "I'm sorry, Trixie. Does the teasing bother you?"

She shook her head. "No, I kind of like it. With you, it doesn't feel barbed."

"It's not," I promised. "And however bohemian my growing up may have been, my mother always insisted on good manners. She considered good etiquette a practice of love."

"Practice of love?"

"It was my mom's philosophy that people's lives are like wheels, turning, spinning, cycling, over and over. And that if we could make love the hub of our wheels, then every spoke coming from it would keep us rolling as smoothly as possible on our paths. She called those spokes 'practices of love.' Selfless acts of goodness that bring light and love into the world."

"I remember you saying that she'd passed away," Trixie said, sadly.

I nodded. "She died while I was locked up."

"I'm so sorry."

"Thank you," I replied.

"It sounds like she was an amazing person. Was she a therapist or something?"

I burst out laughing so hard I started getting looks from the other diners.

She raised an eyebrow. "What's so funny?"

"My mother *saw* a lot of therapists over her lifetime,

but never became one."

Trixie's hand went to her mouth. "Oh, jeez. I'm sorry."

"No, it's okay," I reassured her. "Really. She'd be laughing with us. She had the darkest sense of humor possible."

"Can I ask how she passed, or is that too personal?" she asked.

I opened up my kutte. "You can ask me whatever you want. I told you, I'm an open book."

"That surprises me."

"Why?"

"Aren't guys who've been in *prison*," she whispered, "supposed to be more guarded and pokerfaced?"

"That's how some guys do their time, sure. But for most, talking is the only way to pass the time. After a while, you and your cellie get bored of the same old conversations. Bullshit stories about girls, cars, and whatever half-assed plans we were hatching for after our releases. So, after a while talk starts to turn a little more real. More personal. Pretty soon it just seems like phony two-faced bullshit *not* to be real."

"I'd love to hear about your mother. Not just how she passed."

I nodded. "My mom was the most amazing person you could ever hope to meet. She was funny, beautiful, and up for just about any kind of adventure that came her way. A seeker in every sense of the word. Her interests ranged from Astronomy to Astrology. She was also very troubled. She suffered severely from bi-polar disorder from a young age, which took years to properly diagnose and begin to treat. That mixed with a truckload of childhood trauma, and years of alcohol and drug abuse landed her in and out of mental institutions, rehabs, and drunk tanks through most of her life."

59

"Where was your dad?"

"Who knows? Probably dead or in jail by now. He certainly wasn't around to help raise me. When my mom was having a bad spell or locked up I'd be passed around among whatever friend or family member was available. I slept on more couches, lumpy guest beds, and in sleeping bags on floors than I can count. By the time I was fifteen it was 'three hots and a cot' seven days a week, three hundred and sixty five days a year."

"And then your mother died?"

"She committed suicide while I was serving my third year. An intentional overdose of the multitude of pills she'd been prescribed."

Trixie's eyes filled with tears. "Oh, my Lord, I'm so sorry."

"There had been multiple attempts over the years, but this time she succeeded. A temporary solution with permanent effects."

Trixie placed her hands on mine, and a charge of electricity surged through me. It was the first time our skin had made contact and I was already hungry for more.

I sighed. "I hope I didn't spoil our good time."

"No," she said, reassuringly. "I asked, and I'm really glad you told me. You're so easy to talk to and the more you tell me about yourself, the more I feel I want to reveal to you. That probably doesn't make any sense, but—"

"You don't have to explain. I know exactly what you're talking about."

I couldn't keep my eyes off of her. I tried my best not to stare, but I could barely believe she was actually sitting across the table from me.

"I looked for you, ya know," I said, changing the subject.

"What?"

"After I got out of Lakewood. The second I had access

to a computer I started searching for you. I combed every social media platform, job link database, and school reunion site I could find looking for, and tracking down every Trixie I could find in the country."

"Seriously?" she asked.

"Oh, shit. Does that creep you out?"

"No, no," she said reassuringly. "I just can't believe you even remembered me, let alone looked for me."

"Are you kidding? Of course, I remembered you. How could I possibly forget?"

Trixie studied my face. "What is it with you?"

"What do you mean?"

"How is it that you see me so differently than everyone else?"

"Do I?"

She nodded.

"How so?" I asked.

"Most people treat me like a fragile, sheltered, little pastor's kid. The model child, placed on display for all to see. The living example of my parents' stellar Christian child-rearing."

"I didn't know you were a pastor's kid when I met you."

"Yeah, but you know now and that hasn't changed the way you talk to me. The way you joke around and tease me. The only other person that's ever done that is Gemma, and she's been my closest friend forever."

"Are you tight with your family?"

"With my brothers, yes. My parents have absolutely no interest in getting to know who I am and never have."

"How is that possible? You're amazing."

"You don't know me very well."

"Yes, I do," I said, with a confidence that felt as if it were carved into the stone of my heart. "I knew you were the most special woman I'd ever encountered the first night we met, and I think us being here tonight was meant to be."

Beth returned with our omelets. "One Denver, one Cleveland special," she said as she placed our plates in front of us.

"Beth, if I wasn't married already, I'd take ya as m'bride," I said, my accent now landing somewhere between Yosemite Sam and Foghorn Leghorn.

"Yeah? Well, if half my family wasn't from Arkansas, I might be fooled by your punk ass southern drawl."

Trixie and I locked eyes before we burst out into laughter.

Refusing to break character, I replied, "Good, lady. You have besmirched the noble name of my great grandfather Jedidiah Bartholomew Spikeworth the third, who fought bravely and died at the battle of Anteater."

"Do you mean Antietam?" Beth droned.

I coughed. "Yes, well. We would kindly wish to place an order of your finest pie, if you please."

Beth humored us as we ordered desert and I even thought I detected a slight smile forming in the corners of her mouth by the end.

SEVEN

BURNING SAINTS

Spike

AS WE PLOWED through our late-night feast, we talked as openly as two virtual strangers could. We meandered from topic to topic easily and without awkwardness and I'd finally found someone who liked to talk as much as I do.

"Do you have a job or is biker*ing* your full-time occupation?"

I laughed. "I'm a welder."

"Really? What kind?"

"MIG, TIG, Arc, stick. If you've got two pieces of metal, and I've got some oxyacetylene, I can get 'em joined together."

"I have no idea what any of that means. I guess I meant what kind of jobs do you tend to work on?"

"I'm a one-man shop so I can pick up and go wherever I'm needed. I'm fully licensed, bonded, certified, and have been in business for three years. I've worked at the top of commercial high-rise buildings, welding busted radio towers, and six feet under water, repairing a damaged oil pipeline that was ready to burst."

"I definitely need to keep you away from Gemma. She's always been attracted to danger junkies."

"Keeping me all to yourself, are you?"

Trixie blushed. "No, I'm just trying to save you from her."

"You said the two of you have been friends forever."

"Gemma is a lunatic and the most loyal, honest, generous person I've ever known. She's never even remotely screwed me over, unlike just about every other friend I've had. I never could have gotten through the past few years without her."

"Why's that?" I asked.

"The older I get, the more I butt heads with my parents. My mom especially. And even though I have my own separate apartment, I still technically live 'under their roof.' My job doesn't pay a lot, but I manage to pay for everything, including rent to my parents. It's important to me to be independent and self-sufficient. Gemma comes from money and would love nothing more than to set me up in a posh place overlooking the river, and dress me up in her fancy clothes, but she's never once tried to force her lifestyle on me."

"What does the good pastor's wife think about her?"

"My mother hates Gemma. Says she's a spoiled, bratty, bawdy, godless girl who's always been in need of a good spanking."

"Damn, that's harsh," I said, taking a sip from my

mug.

"No, my mom's totally right, except for the part about needing a spanking." I sighed. "Apparently, she's never found it hard to find someone to help her in that department."

I choked on my coffee.

"Needless to say, I've always kept them apart as much as humanly possible."

"I can see why you had me meet you around the corner."

Trixie frowned. "What do you mean?"

"Well, if your folks are that picky about who you spend time with…one look at me and you'd catch hell for a year."

She shook her head. "That's not it."

"Really?"

"First of all, I'd catch hell for the rest of my life if they saw me with you, but I don't care. I've never really cared what my mother, or anyone else had to say about me."

"What is it, then?"

"I like you, Spike. I liked you the second I met you. And I guess I just don't want to share you. It's why I never told Gemma about you, or my brothers. It's almost like you've been my dream guy for as long as I can remember and if I tell anyone about you, you won't be real." She met my eyes. "That sounds really dumb, huh?"

"Not even a little bit."

"So, now that I've bared my soul, I do need to know your real first name. I know your last name is Kane, but did your mother really name you 'Spike'?"

I chuckled. "It's Jesse."

"Of course, it is."

"You don't like it?"

"No, the problem is, I think I like it a little too much," I admitted. "I was kind of hoping you'd be Myron or

Cletus or something like that to take down the sexiness a little. Unfortunately, I'm just not that lucky in life."

I couldn't stop a laugh.

"So why do they call you Spike?"

"It's kind of a long story and we've been here a while—"

"Oh, no you don't," Trixie interrupted. "I've been waiting since the night we first met to hear the origin story of the mysterious Spike and I'm not going to wait any longer."

I cocked my head. "This whole time we've been getting to know each other, you haven't asked what I did to get locked up."

"Don't change the subject," she protested. "You're supposed to be telling me about your name."

"I am. I promise. The two stories go hand in hand. So how come you haven't asked me why I was in Lakewood?"

"It's none of my business," she replied.

"You've asked plenty of other personal questions, why not that one? Aren't you curious?"

"Of course I am. But I'm also…"

"Afraid of what I did to get locked up?"

She nodded.

"Tell you what." I tapped my fingers on the table. "I'll tell you my story, and at the end of it, if you want me to fuck off down the road, I'll leave skipping."

Trixie laughed. "Now, that I'd like to see."

I leaned back in my seat and exhaled deeply. "I grew up in Vancouver."

"My brother lives in the 'Couve. I love it there."

"Yeah, Most of it's nice, just not where I grew up. My mom worked sporadically at best, so we survived mostly on welfare and "loans" from her mom back in Illinois. As such, the best accommodation we could afford was the

66

Greenway Mobile Estates on Fruit Valley Road. Located between a steel mill and a recycling plant, and just two-hundred-fifty feet from the railroad tracks leading to the nearby train depot."

"Sounds like the lyrics of a country song," Trixie said.

I chuckled. "I happen to know Melody Morgan's guitar player. He's also her old man. Maybe I can pitch them to him."

"Do you, really?"

I nodded. "He rides with the Dogs of Fire, a Portland club we're on friendly terms with. Last year, Ropes sold him a KISS pinball machine that I helped him refurbish, and I got to know him then."

"I don't even know how to process that. I'm the biggest Melody Morgan fan on the planet."

"Well, then I'll make sure you meet her some time."

She smiled, then changed the subject. "What was little Jesse like?"

"I was your basic kid, really. I'd ride bikes with my friends after school or hang out at Franklin Park, which was nearby. I played video games, hopped freight cars—"

"Hopped freight cars?" Her eyes widened. "Were you training to be a hobo or something? Did you have a red bandana tied to the end of stick, to keep all your stuff in?"

"If you keep cracking jokes, I'm never gonna get through this story."

Trixie scrunched up her face. "I'm sorry, I get chatty and goofy when I'm nervous."

"Why are you nervous?"

"Because your childhood sounds dark and dangerous."

"It was, but it was also fun, adventurous, and filled with interesting people. My mom may have been a wreck, but she was also loving, supportive, and mostly really fun to be around. Then there was this other side of her that was volatile, destructive, and untrustworthy. Both sides of her coin were true, and she never tried to hide who she was. She loved everyone she came into contact with. Truly, completely, and without judgement. That instinct got her into a lot of trouble over the years, but she still managed to instill the basic tenants of love in me."

"I wish I could have met her."

"She would have loved you," I replied. "Anyway, one day after school, me and two of my friends were waiting by the tracks for a train we could hop. With the depot being so nearby, the freight trains would be traveling at hoppable speed by the time they reached our neighborhood. Of course, this was illegal, and our parents and teachers were constantly screaming at us to stay away from the tracks, but it was futile. After school, a bunch of us would usually hang out at the park until we heard a train approaching. Then we'd all haul ass for the tracks and see if we could catch a ride home."

"If I'd tried that, I would have been run over, for sure."

"That was a real risk, but not the one we feared the most. The biggest threat to us was Brett MacCourt, better known as Mac of Big Mac. Due to being held back a grade several times, Mac was two years older than anyone in our freshman class. He was a big guy already, but being older made him tower over just about anyone. To top it off, he was mean, violent, and worst of all, rich. He lived a few miles up the road, where Fruit Valley Road turns into Lakeshore, leading to the posh Felida area of Vancouver. Because of our shared proximity, some of the city's richest and poorest kids were thrown together to co-exist at our school. Most of the kids, on either side of the poverty line were totally fine and got along without incident, but some of the more entitled rich kids, like Mac, treated those of us without money like garbage."

"I hate bullies," Trixie growled.

"Bullies, I can handle. Mac was something else. He'd skip sixth period just so he could lay in wait for us at the park, or surprise us at the tracks. He'd jump out of wherever he'd been hiding, grab whoever he could get a hold of, and beat the shit out of them just for fun. He broke Danny Pendergrass's orbital socket, causing him to lose most of the sight in his left eye."

"Oh, my gosh. Why didn't anyone do anything?"

"Danny's parents tried, but Mac's dad threw hush money at them, and after that no one said shit about it. Not the cops, not the school, and least of all not Danny."

"That's horrible."

I nodded. "So, Mac continued to terrorize everyone until the day it was my turn. It was towards the very end of my Freshman year and had been a few months since Mac had fucked with anybody, so my guard was down. I was with my two best friends, Jeff and Phillip, and we were waiting for a train to hop. Mac threw a rock at us from behind, hitting Jeff squarely in the back of the head. At first, I had no idea what had happened. I just saw Jeff drop to the ground and then blood gushing from the back of his head."

Trixie gasped.

"I turned around to see Mac laughing about fifty feet away, still chucking rocks at us as hard as he could. I completely lost my shit. I looked to the ground to find something I could use as a weapon and spotted a rusty, bent, railroad spike lying near the tracks. Before I could think, I picked it up and ran, top speed towards him. I remember the surprised look on his face as I charged him, and then the next thing I remember is being on top of him, smashing his face with the spike. I hit him three times. Broke his nose, his jaw, and he required one hundred and twelve stiches, and three plastic surgeries."

Trixie gasped. "What about Jeff?"

"He got his bell rang pretty good, and required staples to close up his head, but he was okay."

"But you got in trouble," Trixie said.

I nodded.

"But it was self-defense," she hissed. "That boy was throwing rocks at you."

"The school didn't give a single shit about that. They decided to enforce their zero-tolerance policy and expelled both me and Mac, but that would soon become the least of my worries, because then came the cops and the lawyers. Mac claimed that I was the one and only person to hurt anyone that day. He said that I hit Jeff with the railroad spike first, and then when he tried to break up the fight, I attacked him. After that, Jeff was excluded as a witness."

"What about Phillip?"

"The MacCourt family paid him off just like they paid off Danny's family. Next thing I knew, Phillip was somehow relieved as a biased witness, and he moved to Vermont with his family. I've never seen or heard from him since."

"Instead of paying me off, The MacCourts made sure I was the one who was gonna pay. My day in court came and it was the ADA and the MacCourt's family lawyer against my public defender. I got smeared all over the courtroom floor and the judge sentenced me to four years at Lakewood for aggravated assault. Before adjourning, he said I was lucky I wasn't charged as an adult with felony battery, and he would have gladly given me ten years in a maximum-security prison."

I could tell Trixie was fighting back tears.

"By the time I was transferred from County to Lakewood, the rumor mill had blown the story of me hitting a guy with a railroad spike in self-defense up to an epic tale of me beating three guys to death with the railroad spike I carried at all times." I shrugged. "But the story kept most of my fellow inmates from messing with me, so why ruin it with the truth. Everyone at Lakewood called me Spike from day one and that's who I've been ever since."

Tears flowed down Trixie's face.

"Hey, it's okay. Don't cry," I said, cupping her face. "I'm sorry."

"It's not your fault. I just wish I could have been there. I mean, *someone* should have been there to protect you." She bit her lip. "Maybe if I'd known you back then, I could have found help from someone in our church."

"Yeah, I didn't exactly see the line of good Samaritan lawyers lining up to come to my defense back then."

"You're clearly a very strong person to have gone through all of that and end up as great as you have."

"Is that a joke?"

"Not even remotely," Trixie said. "Why would you think that?"

"Most people wouldn't think of an ex-con, biker, welder, covered in tattoos as a guy who's on the winning side of life."

"Who cares what they think? They don't know you, do they? I see a young man who's overcome a ton of adversity, become highly self-educated, learned skills along the way and parlayed them into a thriving small business. Plus, you've built a life for yourself that gives you the freedom to ride and spend time with your adopted club family."

I sank further into my seat. "You really aren't like anyone I've ever met."

"Same goes for you, Spike." She smiled. "What ever happened to your friend that was with you at the dance? Screech, was it?"

"Screek," I corrected.

"Oh, that's right, because his name was Dawson."

I nodded at the bittersweet memories flooding back. "Screek was released about six months after me and was doing okay for a while. But before too long, he started using again, and within a year was incarcerated. Since he was an adult, they sent him to the Oregon State Pen. He'd been popped with a loaded weapon, while dealing, so it was not good." I took a deep breath, steeling my emotions. "He'd always been a wiseass and had only been inside for a matter of months before he popped off to the wrong guy who just happened to be a high ranking member of the Aryan Brotherhood. Screek couldn't stand racists, so I'm sure whatever he said to him wasn't good. In fact, it got him killed."

"What happened?" she asked.

"The guards found him in his cell, he'd been stabbed to death. They were never able to prove who did it."

Of course, what she didn't need to know what that I'd found out who did it, and Ropes and I'd got the nod from Cutter to take care of them, which we did.

"Oh, Spike, I'm so sorry."

"It was a long time ago and he had a lot of demons but he's at peace now," I said, forcing a smile. "Okay, I held up my end of the bargain, now it's your turn."

She cocked her head. "My turn? What are you talking about?"

"Eight years ago, at the dance. I promised you I'd tell you how I got my name, and you promised me a dance."

Trixie giggled nervously. "Wait. You're not serious."

"Of course, I am. I made good, and now I'm owed a dance."

"We're in a Shari's."

"Alright, then. I'll take you someplace we can dance on our next date."

She narrowed her eyes. "Is that your way of asking

72

me on a second date?"

"Is that your way of saying yes?"

Trixie bit her lip and I swear my dick took notice. "I'd love to go out with you again."

"C'mon," I said. Peeling a hundred-dollar bill from my money roll, I placed it on the table before taking Trixie by the hand and leading her out. "Lemme get you home."

"Don't you want to wait for your change?"

"Beth was a good sport," I said, handing my helmet to Trixie. "She deserves a nice tip."

We strolled out arm in arm, and it took every ounce of my strength not to kiss her right then and there. Trixie climbed onto the back of my bike and threw her arms around my waist, and it felt to me like she was exactly where she belonged.

EIGHT

BURNING SAINTS

Trixie

THE NEXT MORNING, I walked into work and settled myself behind the reception desk, powering on the desktop and turning the phones off night mode. I was early so I headed into the kitchen to drop my lunch in the fridge and brew a pot of coffee, arriving back at my desk to find the HR manager waiting for me.

"Hey, Alma," I said. "How was your weekend?"

"It was good. Do you have a minute?"

"Ah, sure."

She smiled but I could tell it was forced. "Come on

down to my office."

My stomach roiled. This wasn't good.

"Am I in trouble?" I asked as we stepped into her office and she closed the door.

"No, of course not." She waved to a chair before sitting behind her desk. "Have a seat."

I lowered myself slowly into the chair and clasped my hands in my lap.

"We have to let you go."

"What?" I squeaked. "Why?"

"The attorneys have decided to have their secretaries take their calls, so we have no need for a receptionist anymore."

"What about the front desk for visitors?"

"We don't get walk-ins and when we have clients, the secretaries will take on those responsibilities."

I wondered how they were all going to feel about that. They already complained about how overworked they were. It was true we didn't get walk-ins, but we did have a busy client list and meetings happened multiple times a day, which required coffee, water, sodas, and often times food ordered in. I took care of it all. However, I had a feeling pointing that out would fall on deaf ears.

"You're receiving a month's severance, and we know you've got vacation time banked, so we're giving you that as well. Also, the COBRA information for your insurance will be sent to your home."

"Okay."

She handed me a check and a thick envelope. "We'll give you some time to pack up your desk, but I'll need your keycard back now."

"It's at the desk, in my purse."

"Right, I'll follow you back."

I nodded and we made our way to the reception desk and I grabbed my purse, handing Alma my keycard. "I don't actually have anything other than these pictures and my lunch here, so I'll just grab those and leave now."

"That'll be fine."

I nodded and gathered my things, making my way to the door.

"I'm really sorry about all of this, Chris," Alma said.

"Are you?" I asked, channeling Gemma to find both my nerve and my audacity.

"I'm sorry?"

"Well, I'm thinking that if you were really sorry, and actually cared one iota about the people who worked here, you wouldn't do a job that consisted of covering the butts of people who make more money than god. Not to mention, you're eliminating the employment of someone who really needs the money, dumping those responsibilities onto people who are already overworked and underpaid. And you know that this is retaliation for coming to you about Dan's pervy comments."

"It absolutely is not," she countered.

"I came to you in confidence, Alma. Asking you the best way to handle a difficult situation." I sighed. "If I were you, I wouldn't be able to sleep at night knowing that I worked for people who let dirty old men keep their jobs over a twenty-two-year-old daughter of a revered and respected local pastor. For your information, I have everything recorded. That's the beauty of cell phones, right? You can actually take them everywhere you go without anyone seeing them."

She let out a quiet gasp.

"So, I'm going to go home and figure out how much money I'm going to take from pervy Dan when I file my wrongful termination lawsuit. Have the life you deserve, Alma. I hope I never see you again."

I turned on my heel and scurried away, pressing the button for the elevator, my heart thumping out of my chest.

Luckily, the doors opened quickly and I stepped inside, grabbing my phone as I waited to be delivered to the parking garage below. I found my car and waited until I was out of the garage before calling Gemma.

"Well, hi there, bestie. To what do I owe this early morning call?"

"I just got fired," I said, guiding my car toward the freeway.

"What the hell?"

"Yep. And you'll never guess what I did."

"Tell me everything."

I filled her in on my morning. Every detail, including what I said to Alma.

"Oh my god, you bad bitch," she crooned. "I'm so proud of you."

"But I couldn't have done any of that without you, Gem. If you hadn't told me to start documenting everything and record all my interactions with Alma and pervy Dan, I'd have no leg to stand on."

"Well, now you do and I have a great solicitor."

"I'm not going to sue them."

"Like hell you're not."

"I don't have that kind of money, Gemma. And they're *lawyers*. I'm pretty sure they'll know every trick in the book to get out of whatever I throw at them."

"Right, love, this is what we're going to do. *I'm* going to pay for the solicitor's time. We pay her a hefty retainer to be on-call and she's done nothing for months, so she's got the time. You can pay me back with whatever you win… or not, I don't give one bloody fuck if you do or you don't, but it's important that men like this can't keep doing this."

I sighed. "Maybe you're right."

"There's no *maybe* about it."

"How about I agree to meet with your attorney and if she thinks we have a case, we'll go from there?"

"I can live with that," she said. "Now, where am I meeting you for brunch? My treat."

I laughed, my heart light again as we decided on a spot to eat. Our choice was back the opposite way I'd just driven, so I headed that way. As I drove, I made a conscious decision not to worry. At least for today.

Tomorrow, however, all bets are off.

* * *

I pulled my car into the garage just as my mother was sliding into hers. "Christine, why are you home so early?"

"I was laid off," I said as I locked my car.

"What did you do?"

"Nothing, Mom, but thanks for your unending faith in me."

"Honestly, Christine. Why do you have to take everything so personally?"

I didn't have the energy to fight with my mother. "They are eliminating my position to save money."

"Well, that must be disappointing. But praise the Lord, He always provides. I'll let your father know you're available to come back and work for him."

"I'm *not* available to come back and work for him," I countered.

"How are you going to pay your rent, small as it is, if you don't have a job?"

"I was given severance," I said. "I appreciate the fact that Daddy has said I always have a place, but I'm going to take a few days before I make any final decisions."

Mom sighed. "Suit yourself."

I gave her a tight smile and headed upstairs, leaning against my door after I'd closed it. I double bolted the lock and attached the chain just in case she tried to barge in again, then I made my way to my bedroom and practically fell onto the bed.

I was only there for a minute or two when my phone rang. I sat up long enough to fish it out of my purse, then flopped back onto the mattress as I answered the call. "Hello?"

"Trixie? You sound different."

"Yes, it's me. Hi, Spike."

"You okay?"

"Yes," I grumbled. "Well, other than the fact I got fired today."

"What the fuck?" he snapped. "What happened?"

"It's not a big deal."

"Talk to me, Trix."

I rolled my eyes and then I spilled. Everything including my issues with pervy Dan, which made him go quiet. Like, so quiet I thought the call had dropped.

"Are you still there?"

"Yeah, I'm here." He cleared his throat. "I'm coming over."

I sat up. "What? Why?"

"You don't want me to come?"

"No, it's not that, but don't you have a job?"

"I'm not working today."

I settled my hand against my stomach. "It's pouring outside, you can't ride in this weather."

"I'm at the Sanctuary. I'll borrow a truck."

I blinked back tears. "Are you saying you'd be willing to stop whatever you're doing and haul your butt all the way over here in order to cheer me up?"

"That all depends."

"On what?"

"Will it cheer you up?"

"Immensely."

"I'll be there in twenty."

He was gone before my phone beeped and I sat on my bed for about ten seconds before his words finally registered.

"Oh, crap, I only have twenty minutes to change!"

I went into overdrive, rushing to find something cute before doing a quick cleanup of my space, including making my bed and emptying the dishwasher.

I'd set an alarm to warn me at the fifteen-minute mark, so when it pealed, I grabbed a jacket and headed downstairs to guide Spike up my long driveway.

He arrived about two minutes early, pulling up in a giant pick-up truck. I pointed to the left side of the driveway which was directly behind my car parked in the garage. He could stay there as long as he wanted without blocking either of my parents' cars.

He slid out of the cab and closed the door, looking unbelievably gorgeous in jeans, motorcycle boots, and a leather jacket.

"Hi," I breathed out.

"Hey. You didn't need to come down, it's freezing."

"I had to show you where to park and finding my place is a little confusing." I smiled. "Come on up."

I led him up the outer stairs and inside, closing the door behind us and it was like my whole world suddenly felt right. I shrugged out of my jacket and faced him. I couldn't stop staring at his face. He was beautiful.

"You okay?" he asked.

"Yes, why?"

"Because you're lookin' at me like you've just discovered chocolate and I'm Willy Wonka."

I licked my lips. "It's just…"

He raised an eyebrow. "It's just what?"

I felt heat creep up my neck. "I really want to kiss you but—"

Before I could get the rest of my sentence out, Spike pushed me gently up against the wall, his hand sliding to my neck and he covered my mouth with his. I sighed, gripping his jacket as I opened my lips, his tongue slipping between them and I opened further to deepen the kiss.

He broke the kiss far too soon, stepping away from me as he dragged his hands through his hair. "Jesus."

I pressed my lips together and cocked my head. "Are you praying or swearing?"

"Not sure," he said, smiling slowly. "All I know is that was fuckin' divine."

"It really was." I let out the breath I hadn't realized I was holding and nodded. "But it also wasn't quite right."

He frowned. "How the fuck was that not right?"

"Kissing you is better than chocolate," I mused. "To be honest, chocolate's not my favorite thing in the world."

"Oh yeah? What *is* your favorite?"

"Cheese," I said on a breath. "Oh my word, yes. It's like I'm dying for cheese and you're the entire state of Wisconsin."

He laughed... a deep belly laugh... before closing the distance between us and kissing me even more thoroughly. "Do you have any idea how beautiful you are?"

I shrugged. "Depends on the day."

"If you ever have a day when you don't feel like the goddess you are, you call me. Immediately."

I laid my palm on his cheek and tapped his face. "Are you for real?"

"Why wouldn't I be for real?"

"Oh, I don't know, because you're this incredibly beautiful man, carved out of stone, looking like Johnny Depp circa nineteen-eighty-seven, and I'm a sheltered, naïve woman who's gained at least forty pounds since you last saw me. I've never dated anyone prettier than me, and I'm not sure how I feel about it."

He was looking at his feet as a I bared my insecurity and I thought he was contemplating my words.

He was not.

I noticed his shoulders shaking and realized he was laughing.

"Are you serious?" I squeaked, stomping my foot. "You're laughing at me?"

"No." His head shot up and he frowned. "Never. I would never laugh *at* you. Especially not about something like this. I'm laughing because you think I'm prettier than you which leads me to believe none of your mirrors work in your goddammed apartment."

"Spike," I hissed out. "Don't be dramatic."

"I'm not being dramatic, baby, I'm being fuckin' serious. You are beautiful and I don't give one rat's ass about what the scales say. You could gain another sixty pounds and you'd still be the prettiest girl in the world."

I reached for his jacket, fisting my hands in the leather, as I tugged him forward. "I need you to kiss me again."

He grinned, obliging me quite thoroughly.

Breaking our connection, he dropped his forehead to mine. "You're gonna need to show me around, honey, or I'm gonna fuck you on your floor."

I bit my lip. "Would now be an appropriate time to tell you I'm a virgin?"

He sighed.

"Sorry, was that bad timing?"

"No," he said. "I had a feeling, but it just makes you even more special because when we finally move to that part of our relationship, it's gonna be permanent."

"You think we'll be permanent?"

"I don't think, Trixie. I *know*." He smiled, kissing me

again. This time, gently and far too quickly. "Now, show me around so I can take a few deep breaths."

I gave him a reluctant nod and led him around my tiny space. It was a short tour, so neither of us really got a chance to calm down.

My father did that. In the form of banging on my door. Spike frowned. "I'll get it."

"I can answer my own door, Spike."

"Whoever it is, sounds angry," was all he said, pulling open the door, and I sighed.

"Hi, Daddy."

"Christine." Daddy turned to Spike. "That your truck in the driveway?"

"It is," Spike said. "Is it in the way?"

"No, not at all," my father replied with all the slickness of a professional Christian. "I was just admiring it. Is that a mid-seventies F-100?"

"A seventy-two. It's a buddy's," Spike said, reaching out his hand. "I'm Spike. It's nice to meet you, sir."

Daddy pointed to Spike's jacket, ignoring his hand. "I take it from your get up there, you ride a motorcycle as well?"

Spike smiled. "Yes, sir. You a fan of classic bikes as well as trucks?"

"No. Not particularly. Too dangerous if you ask me. I always steered my sons away from riding motorcycles." He glanced at me. "Looks like I should have warned my daughter as well."

"Daddy," I admonished.

"Just a joke, angel. I'm sure your friend can take a little friendly ribbing."

"Of course," Spike retorted. "That's why I wear this *get up*. To protect my ribs."

"Well, it's nice to meet you, too, son." Daddy focused back on me, stepping inside which forced Spike to move out of the way.

"Is everything okay, Daddy?" I asked.

"Everything's fine, button. I was just checking on you. Also, your mother wanted to know if you'll be joining us for dinner. Your friend is welcome to join us, of course."

"I'm sure Spike's busy—"

"I've got time," Spike countered.

My father smiled. "Wonderful. Everything should be ready in about fifteen minutes."

"Okay," I said. "We'll see you then." With a nod, my father left us, leaving the door open, and I faced Spike, whispering, "It's a trap."

Spike laughed, closing the door. "How could dinner be a trap? Is your mom a bad cook?"

"No, it's not that." I shook my head. "She doesn't cook, Celeste does. But you're going to get a sermon and they may or may not end it with a makeshift altar call. You'll be put on the spot in ways you've never been before."

He held out his hand, pulling me against him when I took it. "I can handle your parents, Trix."

"God, I hope so," I breathed out.

Sliding his hands around my waist, he gave me a squeeze. "Why are you worried? Concerned a biker can't conversate with your high-class parents?"

"Stop that," I bossed. "In fact, don't ever say anything like that again, got it?"

He raised an eyebrow. "Oh, yeah? How come?"

"It will *never* be me worrying about you." I slid my hands up his chest. "You're perfect just the way you are."

"Then what's the problem, baby?"

I studied my hands resting on his chest. "I'm worried you'll feel they're too much of a pain in the butt to stay with me."

"Look at me, honey."

It took me a second, but I finally felt strong enough to look at him without crying.

"It took me a long time to find you. Your parents aren't going to be the reason we break up before we begin. There ain't anything that's gonna do that because you're it for me."

"You're it for me, too."

He grinned, kissing me gently. "You busy Saturday night?"

I shook my head.

"It's family night at the club. In fact, it's a joint party with the Dogs of Fire, so we're doin' it over at their clubhouse. Wanna come?"

I nodded. "Definitely."

"Pack a bag, it'll be a late night. We'll stay at the club and on Sunday morning everyone will cook up a big ass breakfast together."

I frowned. "I love the sound of Sunday breakfast with you so much, but I can't."

"Why not?"

"Because I have to go to church with my parents on Sunday. It's the price of living here for low rent."

"Right." Spike sighed. "And my girl always follows the rules."

I wrinkled my nose. "I don't *always* follow the rules."

"That wasn't a dig, honey. Just an observation."

"It sounded like a dig," I grumbled.

"Hey, no dig." He cupped my face. "We're different, those differences are gonna clash sometimes. That doesn't mean I'm trying to make you feel bad for those differences, got it?"

I shrugged. "We're so different, Spike. I know next to nothing about the world. I mean, I'm not stupid—"

"Stop," he growled. "Don't ever put you and 'stupid'

in the same sentence, Trixie, or I'll lose my shit. Being sheltered is not being stupid."

I sighed. "Okay. It's just sometimes I feel stupid."

"Well, that's..." he grinned. "Dumb."

"You're lucky you're cute."

He laughed, leaning down to kiss me again just as my phone buzzed on the counter. I read the screen and grimaced. "Dinner's ready."

"It's gonna be fine," Spike said.

"Famous last words, as they say."

He gave me a squeeze and we headed downstairs.

NINE

BURNING SAINTS

Spike

T HE MITCHELL'S HOUSE was impressive
enough from the outside, but the inside was like
something straight out of one of those glossy
home décor magazines. The huge, open-style home was
decorated to the nines, much like one of the two women
standing in the kitchen. And although her back was
turned to me, and it had been eight years since I'd last
seen her, I instantly recognized Sherri Mitchell's bottle-
dyed, fiery red mane.

"You're squeezing my hand," Trixie hiss-pered.

"Oh, shit, sorry," I replied, loosening my grip.

As we approached the kitchen, I could hear Sherri Mitchell giving instructions to the other woman in the kitchen. She looked to be Hispanic, in her early sixties, and she was wearing an apron.

"And please, Celeste, let's double check those water glasses for spots. We don't want a repeat of the dinner with Councilman Beyer, do we?" Sherri asked in a tone that made my flesh crawl.

"Of course, Miss Sherri," Celeste said, with a slight smile and bow.

Sherri Mitchell was dressed from head to toe in yellow and appeared to be wearing jewelry in and on every possible place she could. Earrings, necklaces, bracelets, rings, and to top it all off, a jewel encrusted gold jaguar broach, pinned to the lapel of her well-shoulder-padded jacket.

"Hi, Celeste, you look beautiful," Trixie said as we approached the large island in the center of the kitchen, before going over and giving the woman a huge hug. She then greeted her mother. "Hi, Mom, you look perfect as always."

"Don't be silly," Sherri replied, as if her daughter had told her she looked like a bedazzled banana.

I mean, that's what I was thinking but kept that shit to myself.

"Mom, Celeste, I'd like you both to meet Spike. He'll be joining us for dinner tonight."

"Yes, your father told me," Sherri said, sounding less than thrilled about the news. "Hello, Spike, it's nice to meet you."

"It's wonderful to see you again, Mrs. Mitchell."

Sherri looked to Trixie then back to me with a puzzled expression. "I'm sorry, have we met?"

"Spike was one of the boys who attended the Beach

Blanket dance the church hosted at the end of my senior year."

Sherri paused for a few moments before snapping to. "Yes, of course I remember. All you kids grow up so fast I don't always recognize you, that's all. Were you involved in the Student Ministries group with Christine?"

"I—"

"No, mother. He was one of the young men we were hosting from Lakewood," Trixie said.

"Lakewood Church?" Sherri asked. "I'm sorry, that doesn't ring a bell. Who's your pastor there?"

"Lakewood Youth Correctional Facility," I corrected her.

Sherri's smile dipped. She was far too polished to let it fully drop, but I definitely saw it dip.

Sherri put her hands to her hips. "I thought you looked familiar. You're the one I caught sneaking around the kitchen that night, aren't you?"

"You have an excellent memory," I replied.

"Yes, she does," Trixie said. "So, I'm sure she'll remember that I asked you for help, and that showing up in the kitchen that night was all just a big misunderstanding."

"Why are you talking about me like I'm not here?" Sherri asked.

Trixie chuckled, ignoring her mother's exasperated comment. "Mother, that dance was a million years ago, and I'm a grown adult woman now."

"A fact you've been keen to bring up a lot lately." Sherri was talking to her daughter, but she was staring straight at me.

"All I'm saying is, let's welcome Spike to our dinner table with open, loving, *Christian* arms, shall we?" Trixie challenged.

"Yes, of course," Sherri grumbled.

"Excellent." Trixie's face beamed and I wondered how in the hell it was possible that this woman came from the parents she had. "Spike, I'd like you to meet Celeste. She's the sixth member of our family. She was a second mother to all us kids, and we'd all fall apart without her."

"It's a pleasure to meet you, Señora Celeste," I said, gently taking her hand and kissing it.

Celeste said nothing but turned to Trixie and winked.

"Celeste, whatever you're cooking tonight smells absolutely delicious," Gary Mitchell said, joining us in the kitchen.

"I had Celeste prepare Duck Fesenjān for this evening's meal," Sherri said.

"My God, how He loves me," Gary said, placing both hands over his heart.

"Do you like duck?" Trixie asked.

"I-I've never had it before."

"You'll love it," Gary said. "The way Celeste cooks. It practically melts in your mouth."

"Fesenjān is a duck stew with pomegranate seeds and walnuts," Sherri chimed in.

"I see." I tried to sound sincere as I added, "Sounds delicious."

"Thanks again for joining us this evening, Spike," Gary said.

"Thanks for the invite."

I had a theory that most evangelical Christian pastors fell under one of two basic categories. The father figure, or the fuckable figure. From what I could see, most churches seemed to be led by either an older, slightly out of touch, unassuming dad type, or a hip, young charismatic cool guy. Gary Mitchell clearly fell into category one. He was short, stocky, and wore the moustache of a nineteenth century train conductor.

"Did you take your back pill?" Sherri asked her

husband.

"Yes, dear." Gary replied, before turning to me. "Old sports injury."

"Oh, good grief," Sherri interjected. "You fell out of a golf cart on the ninth hole at a resort in Mexico."

"Can I get you something to drink, Spike?" Gary asked, ignoring his wife's 'jab.'

"Oh, sure," I replied. "I'd love a beer. Any kind'll do, I'm not picky."

"We don't drink alcohol in this house," Gary said, in a slightly less friendly tone. "How about a Fresca? I'll grab some from the basement."

I threw Trixie a grimace and a shrug, as she clearly tried to fight back a laugh.

"Sounds great," I replied.

I couldn't imagine what it must have been like for her to grow up in a place like this. Shit, I had it easy in Lakewood.

"He's going to come back with a scripture about alcohol," she whispered, guiding me into the family room next to the kitchen, but out of earshot of her mother. "Bet you ten bucks."

"Didn't Jesus drink wine with his disciples? And pretty much everywhere else he went? Wasn't his first miracle making sure there was wine at the party?"

She chuckled. "My father would give you an answer about wine being different back in the times of Jesus, and how it wasn't like it is now."

"Was it?" I asked.

She scoffed. "No, of course not, it's wine. It's always been wine. That's what makes it... wine. From a molecular standpoint, things are the way they've always been. You ferment a grape, you get a chemical reaction. It's the same now, as it was at the beginning of the universe."

"So, you're not someone who thinks science is mumbo jumbo, anti-god talk?"

"Of course not. People act like there are good chemicals

and bad chemicals… good people and bad people. Free will or the will of God. One or the other. When in truth, life is about how we handle ourselves within the environment we find ourselves."

"Seems to me that kind of talk would be bordering on heresy for a pastor's kid."

"Bordering nothing," she said. "For a lot of people in my dad's church, they'd want both me *and him* run out on a rail if they ever heard me talk like that."

"Seriously?"

"You really haven't been around religious people, have you?"

"Only at Lakewood," I admitted. "There were a couple of younger guys that would come around and talk to us. Guys that were like us when they were younger but had 'found' Jesus and were looking to pass on whatever it was they found. I don't know, it was always kind of vague and confusing to me."

"How so?"

"They'd talk to us about turning our lives over to Jesus, which never made any kind of sense to me."

"What are the two of you whispering about over there?" Trixie's mother demanded.

"We're talking about what it means to give your heart to Jesus, mother," Trixie retorted.

"I don't know why every question I ask has to be answered with a smart alec remark," she hissed. "If you don't want to tell me, that's fine."

"I can't win," Trixie whispered in exasperation.

Her father returned, handing me a can of Fresca. "You know, scripture tells us in Ephesians chapter five, verse eighteen: 'Do not get drunk on wine, which leads to debauchery.' It's why we have a sober house."

Trixie spun away from her father, fighting back a laugh.

I held my can up to him in a toast. "To the sisterhood

of the temperance movement."

Her dad looked bewildered as he said, "Praise the Lord," before making his way into the kitchen.

I took a sip of the soda and grimaced. "I think offering anyone a Fresca should be a sin."

Trixie grinned. "It is... in the lesser-known book of Libations, chapter one, verse six."

I raised an eyebrow. "The book of Libations?"

She nodded. "It also warns those who thirst of the evils of Monster energy drink and White Claw."

I grinned, sliding my hand to her lower back, wanting to kiss her so badly, I debated taking her into the powder room and fucking her on the floor. I didn't even care if her parents caught us. Maybe they could learn a few things. I doubted they'd fucked since the Bush administration, if they ever did more than the three times to get their kids.

"Stop looking at me like that, Wonka," Trixie hisspered. "My parents will notice."

"So?"

"They'll ban me from seeing you if you keep looking like you want to eat me."

I leaned forward and whispered, "I *do* want to eat you."

She blushed and dropped her head. "Well, you need to control yourself or we'll both be in trouble."

I laughed. "No promises."

"Dinner's ready," Sherri announced, and I followed Trixie to the dining room table.

* * *

Trixie

We moved into the dining room and took our seats. My parents, per usual, sat at the opposite ends of the long table, and Spike and I sat next to each other.

"You have a beautiful home, Mrs. Mitchell," Spike said.

"Thank you, and please call me Sherri," my mother said, using her 'ministry' voice. I could only imagine what she was thinking, and none of it was good.

Once she'd seated us, Celeste disappeared back to the kitchen.

"Have you lived here long?" Spike asked.

"I guess it's been about twelve years since we moved into this house," my father replied. "Before moving up here we had a place in Glenfair."

"I still miss the old house," I said.

My mother rolled her eyes. "Of course, you do."

"I have a lot of great memories of that place." I shrugged. "Besides, us kids grew up in that house."

"Correction, you kids outgrew that house. It started the day we brought you home from the hospital, and the house just got smaller and smaller as you all got older."

"Praise the Lord for providing my family with a home that fits us all now," my father said.

"Jenson and Mattias moved out years ago and I live over the garage," I muttered.

My mother opened her mouth, no doubt to scold me, but I was saved by the arrival of Celeste and our salads.

"And for you, sir," Celeste said, placing a salad in front of Spike.

"Thank you very much," Spike said, before stopping her. "Excuse me, may I ask where you're from originally?"

"I am from Spain. Tarragona."

"That's near Barcelona, right?"

Celeste smiled and nodded.

"In that case, *moltes gràcies*."

Celeste replied, "*Ets més que benvingut. Jove, ets benvingut i molt guapo*," before once again, leaving us.

"Spain?" My mother replied. "I thought Celeste was from Mexico."

"You speak Spanish?" I asked Spike.

"Growing up, my mom's best friend, Toni, was like an aunt to me. She was from Spain and taught me basic conversational Spanish, more specifically Catalan. During my stay at Lakewood, she sent me a book called How to Speak Catalan in a year. It took me two and a half years to get through the book, but I did it."

"That's amazing," I replied.

"Isaac Asimov said, 'Self-education is, I firmly believe, the only kind of education there is.'"

"And who is he?" my mother asked.

My father waived his hand dismissively. "He was a science fiction writer, dear. You wouldn't like his books."

Spike looked stunned. "Asimov was arguably one of our greatest writers, ever. He wrote over five hundred books, and not all science fiction, either. He wrote mysteries, fantasies, and academic books on science, history, math, chemistry, and astronomy. He even wrote a handful of books about the Bible."

"He was an atheist," my father replied.

"Asimov considered himself a humanist and a secular Jew," Spike corrected.

"Fancy ways of saying you're an atheist, aren't they?"

"According to Asimov, Atheism describes only what he didn't believe in, so it was an incomplete description of him."

"And what do you believe?" my father asked.

"Regarding God?"

"You don't have to answer that," I said.

"I don't mind at all," Spike said, turning to my father. "I guess you could say I'm agnostic. I have no idea if there's a god or not. I have no clue if, when we die, we go to heaven, hell, Valhalla, or are reincarnated. I don't know if there are even such things as good and evil. All I know is that there are eight billion people stuck together on this rock, which is orbiting a smaller-than average star, in an unremarkable galaxy, that's all hurtling through time-space at seventy-six-thousand miles per hour. And that since mankind's earliest beginnings, we've tried out a lot of gods, and a lot of religions, and every one of them seems to have divided us more than brought us together."

"There is only one true God," my father said.

Spike smiled. "I hope I haven't offended you."

"What kind of pastor would I be if the words of an unbeliever offended me?"

Spike nodded. "Good."

"You know, Spike," my father said. "Earlier, I called what you're wearing a 'get up,' and I fear *I* may have offended *you*."

Spike smiled and waved my father off. "No offense taken, sir. Really."

"Well, I was doing some research on biker culture in my study while the ladies were preparing tonight's meal, and if I'm right, the vest you wear is called a kutte. Is that correct?"

Spike nodded. "Yes, sir."

"Please, feel free to call me Gary, or Pastor."

My flesh crawled. I'd always hated it when people addressed my father as pastor. Especially when my mother did it. I don't know why. I know it was meant as a title of respect, and even affection, but it always creeped me out.

My father continued, "The MC on your kutte and leather jacket stands for Motorcycle Club, is that right?"

"That's right. I ride with the Burning Saints Motorcycle Club."

"Back in my day, people called them *gangs*, motorcycle gangs."

"Daddy," I protested.

"It's okay," Spike said, giving my hand a quick squeeze under the table. "The Saints are a club, not a gang."

"And what's the difference, if I might ask?"

"I can't speak for what the one-percenters do, but our club is made up of motorcycle enthusiasts who are legally employed, pay taxes, have families, and serve the greater Portland community during what little spare time they have."

"One-percenter? Those are criminal clubs, yes?"

"That's right."

"More specifically, being a one-percenter means your club isn't averse to committing crimes such as, theft, rape, and even murder."

"Daddy, that's enough," I hissed.

I thought my mother might object to words like rape and murder being tossed around at her dinner table, but she said nothing. She glared at Spike like a juror who'd already found him guilty. Nothing had changed in eight years. Sherri Mitchell did not want Spike anywhere near me.

"It's alright, Trixie. Your father has questions. I don't mind answering them if I can."

"*Trixie?*" my mother all but shrieked. "Have you joined this man's biker gang as well?"

"Mother. Spike just told you he's not in a gang." I narrowed my eyes at her in warning. "And Trixie is Spike's nickname for me, which I happen to love."

"I don't understand what your obsession is with refusing to go by the name your father and I gave you," she whined. "First it was Chrissy, which was bad enough, but now it's Trixie?"

"I misheard Christine the night we first met," Spike explained. "I thought she said her name was Trixie, and I guess it just seemed to suit her."

"Have the two of you been in contact with each other since your release?" my mother asked, her tone turning accusatory.

"No, we just happened to bump into each other last week."

Sherri raised an eyebrow. "Oh? And where was that?"

I squeezed his thigh, but his mouth was a fraction of a second ahead of my cue.

"A tattoo shop on Mississippi," he said.

My mother set her utensils down. "Young lady, did you get a tattoo?"

I speared my last crouton with my fork. "Only one, but it covers my entire back."

My mother took a deep breath. "I'm going to assume that was a joke in the style of your particular sense of humor, but rest assured it is not one I share. I also would highly recommend Ephesians 6:1-3 as your Bible study topic for this evening."

Celeste returned with our entrées, which was fortunate for my mother, as I was seriously on the verge of leaping on top of her and stabbing her in the brain with a butterknife. Anything to make her and my father stop being total dickheads to me and my boyfriend.

The word boyfriend somehow slipped into my thought, and I gasped out loud, causing stares from around the table.

"The duck just looks soooo yummy," I said, cheerily.

I was just getting to know Spike, and while we certainly weren't hiding our feelings for each other, he was far from being my boyfriend. Or was he? Did I want him to be? What did he want? Questions raced through my mind, each more complicated than the one before it.

"Yes, it does," my father said. "Let's eat."

"We can take this time as an opportunity to change the subject," my mother said.

"Which subject would that be, mother?" I asked.

"All of them," she replied.

TEN

BURNING SAINTS

Spike

I MANAGED TO make it through the meal mostly unscathed, except for my right thigh, which was bruised and sore from Trixie's fingertips digging into it the entire time.

"I'm sorry," Trixie mouthed as we pushed in our chairs.

I smiled wide, genuinely unfazed by her parents' questions and assumptions. They didn't treat me any differently than a thousand others I'd encountered since getting out of Lakewood and patching into the Saints. At least this interrogation was polite and came with dinner and dessert.

"Before the two of you go on with your evening, I was wondering if you wouldn't mind joining me briefly in my study, Spike," Gary called from the other side of the dining room. "I'm a bit of a history buff and I have a few items in my personal collection that I think may interest you."

"Can you show Spike all your old dead guy battlefield stuff another time?" Trixie protested.

"It's okay," I assured her, quietly. "I think your father would like to have a man-to-man chat with me." I turned to Gary. "I'd love to see your collection."

"Great," he said, smiling.

"Yippee, more Mommy and me time," Trixie grumbled, before leaving me with her father.

Gary pointed to one of the decorative wooden panels which ran from floor to ceiling all around the dining room. "This way," he said, pressing gently on the panel which revealed itself to be a hidden door leading into his study.

"I thought hidden doors and secret passages were only found in black and white monster movies and Scooby-Doo cartoons," I said.

"What can I say? Channel 36 was a big part of my childhood."

Gary's study looked like a set from an Indiana Jones movie. Volumes of leather-bound books filled towering cases. Old maps from around the world hung in ornate frames, along with antique hunting and exploring gear. Everything in the room, from the furniture to the bearskin rug screamed, "I am a *man*."

"What do you think?" Gary asked, clearly proud of his den.

"It's nice," I replied, glancing at the walls. "These

maps all the places you've been to?"

"Some of them. Others are locations our church has set up ministry centers that I haven't gotten the opportunity to visit yet."

"What's a ministry center?"

"Our ministry centers range from anything to churches, medical facilities, and schools. We currently have twelve set up around the world, with plans to add another eight over the next five years."

"And the people who go to your church pay for all that?"

"Any congregation member or visitor to our church is free to donate to the Lifesprings Church World Services fund should the Lord prompt them. And I'm happy to say that giving has risen tenfold over the twenty years since we've been a part of the ministry."

"Your church must be full of some pretty charitable people," I said, pointing to the surroundings. "I do a lot of work for people in this area. I know what these homes cost."

Gary smiled. "The Lord has been generous with his blessings for sure, but I haven't drawn a salary from the church for many years. My family and I have benefited from my bestselling books, which I'm happy to say, keeps the lights on here at Casa Mitchell."

"But you still preach?"

"Writing has been a blessing for sure, but preaching is what God has called me to do."

"I see," I said, but I didn't have a single fucking clue what he meant.

"What about you?" Gary asked. "You mentioned you do work in the area. What line of work are you in?"

"I'm a welder. Mostly freelance commercial work, but I also do custom jobs. I've designed and built gates, railings, and staircases for a handful of your neighbors over the years."

"That's just wonderful, son," Gary said, condescension dripping from his voice.

"Those of us who find our calling in life are pretty lucky."

"I prefer the word blessed. And to God be the glory."

I gave Gary a short nod.

"Would you excuse me, please while I visit the restroom. Feel free to take a look around the study," he said, before disappearing through a side door.

Gary's study was filled with a mixture of historical and religious books, and many that seemed to blend the two topics. The subject of Christian Archeology seemed to be his main focus, based on his reading habits.

Equally as eclectic was his collection of artifacts. Pieces ranging from civil war battlefield finds, such as a confederate soldier's belt buckle, and a union captain's knife, to a tattered piece of cloth enclosed in a glass case. On the case was a small brass plate which contained an engraving claiming the cloth to have come from the uniform of a Roman soldier who was present at the crucifixion of Jesus Christ. How a thing like that could be verified, let alone true, is beyond me, but there it was. Then came the modern era of the exhibit, which tilted heavily toward the JFK assassination. Framed newspaper clippings, photos, and "official" documents hung around a miniature diorama of Dealey Plaza in downtown Dallas, Texas, where the president was shot.

Gary came back in just as I was looking at it.

"Did you make this model yourself?" I asked as he approached.

"Every car, person, tree, and bird you see was lovingly and patiently painted by me."

"Cutter, our club's founder and president, would have loved this place."

"*Would have*? Is he no longer with us?"

I nodded. "Cutter passed away shortly after I became a prospect."

"I'm sorry to hear that."

I smiled. "You'd probably find it hard to believe, but the two of you would have gotten along."

"Why would I find that hard to believe?"

"I don't get the impression you or Mrs. Mitchell care much for bikers."

"I don't know if I'd say that." Gary turned from me slightly and it was then I spotted traces of white powder in his moustache. Looking at him closer I could also see he was sweating, and his pupils were pinned. This man was jacked up.

"Okay then, maybe it's just that you don't like me," I said.

Gary scoffed. "I don't know you well enough to dislike you."

"You know me enough to know that you don't want me around your daughter."

Gary cocked he head. "Do you have a child?"

"No."

"When you have a daughter, you worry when the mailman walks on the same side of the street as her. Seeing my daughter looking at a man like you the way she does is more than a little concerning to me."

"So, this is one of those 'What are your intentions with my daughter?' speeches. Is that it?"

Gary shrugged. "For lack of better terms, let's just call it that."

"To be one hundred percent honest with you, sir. My intentions are to pursue your daughter with everything I have within me. I plan on captivating her heart and earning her trust by being everything she needs me to be. I plan on proving to her every day that I'm a man who is worthy of her love, and on the days when I'm not, I plan on improving until she's as happy as she can possibly be. And then, once I've earned her love, respect, and trust I'll ask her to marry me. And, if I'm the luckiest sonofabitch ever, she'll say yes, and I can prove myself to her until we're too old to chew or screw."

"Does my daughter feel the same way about you?"

"I don't know. In fact, I've just told you more about how I feel about her than I've told her. But you asked my intentions so there they are."

"And how does a guy like you plan on supporting someone like my daughter?"

"I don't know. I'm not interested in someone *like* your daughter. I'm in love with *your* daughter. And I would support her the same way I support myself now."

"As a welder?" he asked.

"That's right."

"And not through criminal activities, because as you said earlier, the Burning Saints aren't one-percenters." He narrowed his eyes. "Right?"

I nodded. "Our club roster is populated by legitimate local business owners."

Gary chuckled. "Legitimate. That's a word only criminals use."

"There's nothing more legitimate than a tax return. I cleared one-hundred-twelve grand last year, and I've only been in business for four years. Not to mention, I've managed to save eighty percent of my income over the past six years, much of which is invested in low risk-high yield money market accounts, savings bonds, and treasury bills."

"Don't try to con me. We both know the Burning Saints aren't a Boy Scout troop. Your club may be all about toy drives and community carnivals these days, but I know your club's history all too well, and it's nowhere near as ancient as the artifacts in this room."

"You're right. My club has a history of violence and perhaps even some criminal activity, but that's not the club I've come up in. Minus, our president, runs a clean shop. No exceptions. And anyone who doesn't fall in line is out."

"I put my faith in God. Forgive me if I don't have much left for your word."

"Don't judge me based on what other people in my club may or may not have done in the past. Do you vouch for everything that happens at all these ministry centers?" I asked, pointing to the maps. "You said yourself, you haven't even visited them all."

"Traveling is difficult for me. My weekly job at the pulpit keeps me pretty busy as you can imagine."

"Does it?"

"I beg your pardon?" he asked, sounding a bit stunned.

"To be honest, and I mean no disrespect to you, I've always imagined a preacher's job as a relatively cushy gig."

"Cushy," he said, visibly struggling to maintain his composure.

"Sure," I continued. "You've got six days to write a twenty-minute book report on one small section of a book you've read a dozen times. Then the day of the oral presentation, you throw in a few jokes you picked up at the last pastor's conference, a few analogies pulled from your high school sport glory days, and with a little help from the watered-down rock band behind you, you can pull a solid C-plus to a B-minus every week. And that's enough to keep the tithers coming back, Mrs. Pastor happy, and for God to stick your report card up on his heavenly refrigerator."

Gary glared at me. "I'm not afraid of you."

"Good. I don't want you to be. I want us to be able to speak freely, man to man."

"How's this?" he retorted. "I want you to stay the hell away from my daughter. I don't know what kind of phase she's going through, or why she's attached herself to you, but it ends tonight."

"I'm gonna assume it's your 'back pills' that are doing the talking right now, and cut you some slack, but don't ever tell me what I can and cannot do again. The same goes for Trixie. She's not your property, your live-in servant, or one of your church drones. She's a grown woman and she can do whatever the hell she wants."

Gary was shaking with anger. "Get out of my house."

"Thanks for the wonderful evening," I said with a smile before pausing. "Oh, and you missed a little," I said, motioning for him to brush his moustache.

His face turned bright red as he quickly wiped away the powder. Now I knew where Trixie got her tendency to blush, but she looked way better than her old man when she did.

* * *

Trixie

Thursday, I got an impromptu invitation for dinner from Mattias and his partner, Ronnie. Instead of texting him back, I called.

"Well, hi there, baby sister, to what do I owe the pleasure?"

"What do you mean?" I asked. "You just texted me."

"Yeah, but you normally just text me back. When's the last time we actually talked on the phone?"

"Fair," I admitted.

"So, what's up?"

"Um, well, I'd *love* to come to dinner..."

"But?"

I bit my lip. "Can I invite someone, please?"

"Is it this boy that Mom and Dad are absolutely apoplectic about?"

I sighed. "They told you?"

"Please, they don't tell me anything. Jens told me."

"Was he kind, or did he pound on his chest, spouting something like, 'I am a big man and my little sister is dating a big ol' tattooed biker. Grrr.'"

Matty burst out laughing as I lowered my voice and imitated our brother warmly and accurately.

"It's like you know him or something," he said.

I smiled. "Weird how that is."

"You can invite whomever you like."

"Okay thanks. I'll let you know if he can make it. I'll text you as soon as I know, but either way, I'll be there."

"Okay, sissy. See you soon."

I hung up and texted Spike. He responded almost immediately with a thumbs-up and I rolled my eyes. That wasn't really an answer to my question so I called him but this time it took a little bit before he answered. "Hey, baby."

"Hi, honey. Um, does thumbs-up mean you want to come with me to dinner or that you acknowledge you got my message?"

He chuckled. "It always means I want to go wherever you go."

"You're not busy?"

"Never too busy for you."

"Matty and Ron are super sweet. Nothing like my parents. Not even like Jens."

"Baby, I'm not worried."

"Okay."

"Pick you up at six?"

"Perfect," I breathed out.

"See you then."

We rang off and I headed into the shower.

* * *

My brother lived in a gigantic home in Felida. It was more home than he and Ron needed but it was far enough away from my parents that they wouldn't visit, and that was really all he cared about (his words, not mine).

Kind of wonky logic, really, considering he lived less than thirty minutes from us, but there was something about Portlanders and their aversion to crossing the bridge into Vancouver, and my parents certainly fell into that bucket.

At least, I liked to think that was the reason why they didn't visit my brother and not because he was gay. Although, I feared it was the latter.

"Nice digs," Spike said as he walked with me to the front door.

"Right? I love their house. It's all warm and cozy. My home away from home."

I rang the doorbell, but it was just a cursory ring because I walked in without waiting for anyone to answer. "We're here!"

Mattias walked out from the kitchen and pulled me in for a bear hug. "Oh my god, sissy, you look amazing."

"I do?"

"Yes, you do," Spike said.

"Oh, this is the man," Mattias said with a grin, going in for a hug.

I tensed slightly but shouldn't have worried. Spike took it all in stride, letting my brother wrap his arms around him. Spike gave Matty's back a quick slap and disengaged quickly, smiling as he stepped closer to me.

"Well, what a man you are," Mattias crooned.

"Mattias, are you flirting?" Ronnie called out.

"I would *never*."

Ron joined us, rolling his eyes as he reached his hand out to Spike. "Ignore him. I'm Ron."

"Spike." He shook Ron's hand and then Ron hugged me.

"Hey there, beautiful."

"Hi yourself." I smiled up at him. "Please tell me you cooked."

"Rude," Matty admonished.

"Self-preservation," I retorted.

"Of course I cooked." Ron chuckled. "Come on in."

"Can I get you something to drink?" Mattias asked.

Spike looked my way. "Ah…"

"Beer?"

"Oh, thank god," he rasped.

"Did Gary have a Fresca at the ready for you?" Ron asked.

"Of course he did," I said. "Followed up with a verse about the sins of drunken debauchery."

Matty handed Spike a beer. "Glass?"

"Bottle's great," Spike said, twisting off the top.

"Wine, sis?"

"Yes, please, red if you have it."

"Do I have red?" He scoffed. "I'm not an animal."

"That was really more of a rhetorical question."

The doorbell pealed just as he handed me a glass of my favorite red and I raised an eyebrow.

"Jens."

"You got Jenson to drive over the bridge?" I asked.

"What can I say?" Matty bragged. "I have all the power."

"Ooh, let me get it," I begged, and Matty waved me to the door.

I set my wine down and rushed to the door, pulling it open. "Ah-huh! Surprise!"

Jenson chuckled, pulling me in for a hug. "Hey, sissy."

"You don't seem surprised to see me." I met his eyes. "Why aren't you surprised?"

"Because I knew you'd be here." He walked in, removing his jacket and hanging it on the hook by the door.

"You did?"

"I did."

"I hate it when you two conspire against me," I grumbled as we headed into the kitchen.

"Conspiring to spend time together over kick-ass food cooked by Ron? Yeah, sure, we'll go with that."

I wrinkled my nose. He had a point, but still. As the baby sister, I had a serious case of FOMO most of the time when it came to my brothers and often felt like I was left out of the conversation. Silly, I know, but true all the same.

He wrapped his arm around my shoulders and kissed the top of my head before greeting the rest of the men.

Jenson did seem surprised to see Spike, but he was polite to him so I relaxed as we all sat down to eat, setting my hand on Spike's thigh, and linking my fingers with his under the table.

"Ron and I have an announcement," Mattias said just as we took our first bite.

"You don't want to wait until dessert, babe?" Ron asked.

"I'm too excited."

Ron shook his head as he smiled.

"What's up, Matty?" Jenson asked.

"We're having a baby."

"Like, literally?" Jenson teased.

We all chuckled and Matty threw a dinner roll at his head. Jenson didn't duck in time, and it hit him square in the forehead.

Matt had been the pitcher on his high school baseball team, and had gotten a full ride to Portland State, so it was no surprise Jenson hadn't seen it coming.

"We found a surrogate," Ron explained. "She's at the four-month mark, and healthy, so we felt it was safe to finally tell everyone."

"Oh my gosh!" I exclaimed, jumping up and hugging my brother first, then Ron. "I'm so excited for you both. You're going to be the best dads."

Jenson followed my lead and we spent the next few minutes congratulating the happy couple before sitting down again to finish dinner.

To say it was one of the best family nights was an understatement, and to have the love of my life to share in the joy was the cherry on top of an already perfect sundae of an evening.

ELEVEN

BURNING SAINTS

Trixie

SATURDAY NIGHT, FOR family night, Spike picked me up a little early, because I wanted to stop by Fred Meyer for wine. However, I was surprised to see he'd brought his bike.

"Hey, baby, you look cute," he said when I answered the door and right before he kissed me.

"You do too," I said, taking in his dark jeans, motorcycle boots, and leather jacket. "I thought we were going to the store."

"We are."

I slid my hands up his chest and raised an eyebrow.

"We're carrying wine on your bike?"

"Yeah. I've got saddlebags. You'd be surprised how much they hold."

"What if I want to get a pie?"

He smirked. "You don't need to get a pie. You don't even need to get the wine. It's a family night. Everything's covered."

"I can't come to a party empty handed, Spike. My grandmother would fly down from heaven and smack me upside the head."

He chuckled. "Well, then we better get goin'."

"Do I look okay?" I asked, my insecurity on eleven.

"You look beautiful."

"Are you sure?"

He cupped my face. "Yeah, I'm sure."

I wrinkled my nose. "But it's not like you're the type to say, 'Hey, Trixie, you should change because those jeans make you look fat,' are you?"

"Baby, what'd we say about you calling yourself fat?"

"It's hypothetical."

"Don't fuckin' care if it's in a dream, you knock that shit off."

I rolled my eyes and huffed out, "Fine. I'll rephrase."

"Don't," he ordered. "You look gorgeous. So gorgeous in fact, I'm having a hard time not stripping you naked and fucking you on your floor."

I let out a quiet gasp and gripped the edges of his jacket. "Don't say things like that."

"Why not?"

"Because I want it too and it makes it harder to resist you."

"So, don't resist me." He grinned, leaning down to kiss me, and I looped my arms around his neck, slipping my fingers into his hair.

I sighed against his mouth, forcing myself to break the

connection, dropping my head to his chest. "You make things impossible, Mr. Kane."

"I'm wearing you down, Ms. Mitchell."

I met his eyes. "I'm not that much of a challenge, Spike."

"I'm a patient man, baby, and you're worth the wait."

"Even if you have to wait until marriage?"

"I'll marry you tomorrow, Trixie, don't doubt it."

"Well, as sweet as that is, it's not going to happen."

"I'm aware." He smiled gently. "I'll wait as long as it takes."

"Really?"

"Really," he avowed, kissing me again. "But we need to go or I'm gonna fuck you on your floor."

I nodded, grabbing my jacket, and following him out the door.

* * *

Pulling into the parking lot of an auto body shop called 'Big Ernie's,' Spike backed his bike into a space near the side door and turned off the engine. "Go ahead and climb off, baby."

I did so, rather gracefully, if I did say so myself. Of course, he'd had to give me a full tutorial on my first ride with him, but we weren't going to mention the colossal failure that was (at least, in terms of me getting off the bike).

He put the kickstand down and climbed off, removing his helmet before helping me with mine. "You good?"

"I'll tell you when you hand me my bag so I can check my hair and makeup."

He chuckled, opening one of his saddlebags, and pulling out my purse and our purchases. I found my mirror and turned toward the flickering light on the outside of the building to check my appearance. I groaned. I not only had helmet head, but helmet face.

"Oh, crap, I look like a chipmunk with a nut allergy."

My cheeks were puffy and splotchy and my eyes were watery from the cold.

Spike laughed. "You look adorable."

"Hold this, please." I handed him the mirror, adjusting his hand so I could fix my face and hair with both hands.

"Baby, you look great."

"Hush," I admonished. "I could be wearing a burlap sack and you'd tell me I looked great."

"Well, you're beautiful."

I met his eyes briefly and scoffed. "I appreciate your adoration, but it's misguided at the present moment, because we're about to *meet your family*."

"Trixie, they're gonna love you."

"I want to make a good impression and walking in looking like a demented squirrel is not a good start."

"I thought it was a chipmunk in need of an epi-pen."

"Semantics, Jesse, semantics."

He grinned. "Love hearing my name outta your mouth, baby."

I took the mirror from him and dropped it into my purse with a smile. "I'll do it more often then," I promised, standing on my tiptoes to kiss him.

I tried to pull away, but he was faster, tugging me forward, and kissing me again, this time much deeper, and rather frustrating.

"You're going to make me forget my manners," I breathed out.

"One can hope."

I wrinkled my nose and patted his chest. "You're lethal, you know that, right?"

"Only to you, baby."

I rolled my eyes. "Keep telling me that."

He chuckled. "I'm a one-woman man, Trix. You never have to worry about that."

"I'm not worried. At least, not today. That might change when PMS hits, but you won't have to guess when that happens."

"No?"

I shook my head. "I'm a little emotional around that time of the month, so it won't be hard to guess."

He smiled. "I'll be ready with wine and chocolate."

"Oh my word, stop."

"No." He kissed me again. "I'm wearing you down."

"Spike!" someone called and he sighed.

"Comin'!" he called back, giving me a squeeze. "You ready?"

"Not in the slightest."

"They're gonna love you."

"I hope so," I whispered, and he took my hand, lifting it to his lips to kiss the palm.

"You need more time?"

"No, I'm good." I squared my shoulders and squeezed his hand, then we headed inside.

We entered a large common room already packed with people. The space was filled with sofas, over-stuffed chairs, a pool table, giant flat-screen television, several smaller tables that a few of the younger children gathered around for board games. There were three pinball machines set up against the wall and bells were dinging as the older kids engaged in epic battles.

My senses were on overload. The smell of alcohol and barbeque wafted through the air, while a low din of gruff male voices mixed with kids squealing in excitement and women laughing with unabandoned joy. In all the churches and religious meetings I'd attended, I'd never once seen a group of people who seemed more alive. They spoke openly and freely about things that would make sailors blush, but also appeared to love just as honestly.

"Wow," I breathed out.

"Yeah," Spike said with a chuckle. "The Dogs' space is cool, right?"

"Yes. Is your clubhouse like this?"

"It's getting there." He smiled. "Let's drop our stuff off in the kitchen, then I'll introduce you."

I nodded and followed him through a door to our right. Several women and a long-haired man were in the kitchen preparing food. Well, the women were. The man was groping a particularly beautiful blonde woman.

"Hatch, love, I'm going to shove this pie in your face, if you don't stop," she warned in a sweet British accent.

Hatch chuckled. "Kinky."

"Hi Spike," the other blonde said in greeting.

"Hey, Cricket. Hatch, Maisie." He set our offerings on the large metal island. "This is Trixie."

Cricket's eyes widened and she grinned. "Oh my god, you're Trixie? Devlin wasn't kidding when she said you were gorgeous."

I blushed and leaned closer to Spike.

"Cricket's our president's old lady," he explained. "Where is Minus?"

Cricket nodded to her right. "Changing a diaper."

"Nice," Spike said, giving my hand a squeeze. "There's a kids' room just down the hall."

"Wow, you have everything covered."

Maisie smiled. "We try. Although, we're going to need to add on to accommodate all the new recruits and families." She tugged on Hatch's beard. "*Aren't* we?"

"Yeah, Sunshine, gettin' right on that."

Maisie rolled her eyes and Cricket laughed. "We do have brothers who do construction, Hatch. You don't need to be part of this... at *all*."

"Who's payin' for it, baby sister?" he challenged.

"There's no need to get facts in the way of this conversation."

"What conversation?" A tall man with yet another epic beard walked into the kitchen, wrapping an arm around Cricket.

"Adding on to the club," Cricket explained. "You also don't need to be part of it."

He smirked. "No shit. I'm not payin' for it."

Hatch tipped his beer bottle toward him before taking a swig.

"Hush," Cricket hissed. "Now, don't be rude. Spike's brought a guest."

"Hey," he said.

"Hey, yourself." Spike grinned. "This is Trixie. Trix, this is our prez. Minus."

"Well, fuck me," he said. "Spike found you."

I chuckled. "He did indeed."

"At Dev's shop, no less," Spike said.

Minus raised an eyebrow. "No shit?"

"My brother, Jenson, works there."

"Jesus, seriously?" He turned his back and lifted his cut and shirt, revealing a large back tattoo. It looked like a club logo of some kind, but interspersed with dates and names, including Cricket's. "He did this."

I gasped. "Wow, I had no idea he could do that. I mean, I know he's an amazing artist, but transferring it to skin is a whole other story."

Minus faced us again with a nod. "Agreed."

"You kids go and get yourselves some food and drinks. Everything's out back," Maisie said.

"Can I help with anything?" I asked.

"No, love, you go and have fun."

"Thanks, Maisie," Spike said, and led me to a giant sliding glass door which was open. Outside, there were five picnic tables, where people were already sitting down and eating.

Two men manned the grills up against a chain-link fence, and there were coolers up against the wall of the building. Each one was labeled so you knew what you were getting. Spike opened the one labeled, 'BEER,' and asked me what I wanted.

"Soda's good," I said, making my way to that particular cooler.

Spike took a few minutes to introduce me to the men at the grills. One of them was Ropes, who I knew was Devlin's husband. The other was Knight, a Dog, whose wife, Kim, was apparently inside dealing with their kids.

"Burger, dog or steak?" Ropes asked.

"Burger, please," I said at the same time Spike said, "Steak."

Ropes had just handed us plates when Devlin walked outside. "Oh my god, hi, Trixie." She walked over to me and hugged me tightly. "Did you quit your job yet?"

I chuckled. "Actually got fired."

"Shut the fuck up."

"Sadly, it's true."

Devlin frowned. "What the fuck happened?"

I gave her the Reader's Digest version and she scowled.

"You need to get Sweet Pea on that. Sue those fuckers."

I glanced at Spike and he said, "Sweet Pea and Callie are both lawyers. Might be a good idea to sit down with them."

"My bestie has a lawyer on retainer and wants me to speak with her first," I said.

"Before you make that decision," Devlin said. "I wasn't kidding about offering you a job. I pay well and you get full medical benefits."

"Really?" I asked.

"Yeah. Wanna come in this week and chat?"

"I would love that. Let me just make sure Jens is okay with his baby sister following him."

She chuckled. "Fair enough. But if he gives you trouble, let me know. I'll set Ropes on him."

"Like hell you will," Ropes countered. "He's doin' a back piece for me next week and I'm not jeopardizing that."

"Don't worry." I grinned. "I can fight my own battles."

Devlin laughed. "I'll get your number from Spike and we'll go from there."

"Sounds great," I said, and followed Spike to one of the empty tables.

We were halfway through our meal when a tall, model-gorgeous woman stormed outside and straight over to Knight. "The asshole is breaking the lease."

"Why?" Knight asked.

Kim cocked her head. "Does it matter?"

"Is he paying the fee?"

"Of course he's paying the fee," she said in a huff. "He knows who I'm married to."

"Then what's the issue?"

"The issue, *Aidan*, is that now I have to find another tenant and it's virtually impossible to find good ones."

"Trixie's lookin' for a place," Spike said.

"Spike," I hissed, mortified that he'd butted in.

Spike smiled. "Sorry, didn't mean to interrupt."

The woman stepped over to us. "Are you Trixie?"

I nodded, wiping my hands before holding one out. "Hi."

"Hi. I'm Kim." She nodded toward Knight. "I'm married to the giant god over there."

I glanced at Spike. "I don't actually know if I can

afford a new place. Where is it?"

"In the Pearl."

I let out a quiet snort. "Um, no, I definitely can't afford anything in the Pearl."

"Yes you can," she countered.

"I don't have a job."

"You will," Spike said. "Devlin's hiring you."

"You don't know that," I countered. "I might not be right for the job. I don't want to make commitments I can't keep."

"Will you fill out an application anyway?" Kim asked. "Spike can bring you by the place next week. The guy I have in there is supposed to be out by Thursday."

"I don't know—"

"We'll come by on Friday," Spike said. "I'll text Knight and set it up."

Her face lit up with a smile. "Perfect."

She walked away and I narrowed my eyes at Spike. "I can't afford my own place yet, Spike. I certainly can't afford somewhere in the Pearl."

"You can, baby. Swear to god. I'll explain later."

I rolled my eyes but decided not to push him on it. It was all a pipe dream anyway and he'd see that sooner than later. Tonight I wanted to enjoy myself, and arguing with a man who could outwit me was not on the agenda.

He gave me a Cheshire grin, obviously thinking he'd won the argument, but I smiled right back knowing he was dead wrong.

* * *

About an hour later, I was sitting on one of the sofas by the fire when the cutest little girl toddled up to me and hauled herself onto the couch beside me. She must have been about four or five and she had a head full of blonde curls and giant blue eyes. "Hi."

I smiled. "Hi, sweetie. What's your name?"

"Chawie."

"Hi, Charlie, I'm Trixie."

She patted the arm of the couch and studied me before sitting up on her knees. "How old are you?"

"Twenty-two. How old are you?"

"Five."

I grinned. "Wow. You're a big girl now."

She bobbed her head up and down. "Who's your old man?"

"My old man?"

"Me," Spike said, sitting between us.

She frowned. "No, you're not."

"Yeah, baby, I am," he insisted.

Her eyes filled with tears and she shook her head. "No. You. Aren't. You're mine."

"Baby girl, I'm way too old for you."

"But..." Her bottom lip quivered as giant tears slid down her cheeks.

A giant, Viking-looking man stalked over to us and demanded, "Why the hell is my daughter crying?"

She reached her arms up and squeaked, "Daddy?"

He picked her up and held her close. "What happened, baby?"

"Spike is *my* old man, not hers." She pointed to me when she said, 'hers,' before burying her head in her dad's neck. "I'm his old wady."

"Sweet Pea, this is Trixie," Spike said as he stood, holding his hands out.

"Hi," I said, giving him an awkward wave.

"Hey, sweetheart. Nice to meet you." Sweet Pea shifted Charlie and the second she saw Spike's open arms, she pitched herself toward him.

"I didn't mean to make you cry, baby," Spike said,

holding her close. "But I'm gonna marry Trixie, honey, so she's always gonna be my old lady. I promise you'll have your own old man someday who'll be better than me."

"No." Charlie wrapped her arms around his neck and shook her head. "Mine."

Sweet Pea rolled his eyes and I bit back a smile as the little girl tried to lay claim to Spike.

A tall, blonde woman joined us, kissing Spike's cheek before wrapping her arms around Sweet Pea's waist.

"Hey, Callie," Spike said.

"Hi, honey." She nodded toward her daughter. "You've just given her exactly what she's wanted all week, you know that right?"

"What?" Sweet Pea asked.

"All she talks about is Spike, honey."

"Not to me, she doesn't."

"Well, you're not a girl," she said.

I decided I was done sitting, so I rose to my feet and Spike introduced me to Sweet Pea's wife.

"Oh, I see why she's freaking out," Callie murmured, laying her hand on Charlie's back. "Baby, why don't we go see what the other kids are doing? I think they've got a movie playing in the playroom."

Charlie held Spike tighter and he made a coughing sound. "Choking me, baby."

"Okay, sweetie, let's go play with the other kids," Callie said, and Charlie raised her head to pout at her mother.

"No. I'm his old wady."

"No, baby," Callie countered. "Trixie's his old lady."

Charlie dropped her head back and burst into tears.

"And the Oscar goes to…" Callie shook her head. "Alright, that's enough, young lady. Come with Mommy. It's time for an attitude adjustment."

Callie managed to wrangle Charlie from Spike, carrying her away as Sweet Pea followed. Spike sat back on the sofa, pulling me onto his lap and kissing me quickly.

"Just how long has this been going on?" I asked.

"What?"

"This unrequited love of Charlie's?"

He shrugged. "No clue. I didn't even know it was a thing."

"Oh dear." I sighed. "There's no telling how many more there are, then."

Spike laughed. "You could be right."

"My man." I gripped his chin. "Breaking hearts all over town."

"As long as I don't break your heart, I don't give a shit about the others."

"Charmer."

He grinned, giving me a squeeze. "You gonna avoid the subject at hand?"

"What subject?"

"Kim's place."

I slid off his lap and sighed. "I can't afford a place in the Pearl, Spike. Period. Even if I get the job with Devlin, it'll still be a receptionist's salary."

"Kim owns that place outright and discounts it heavily for club people," Spike said. "She'll make sure you can afford it."

"I'm not a beans and rice kind of girl," I pointed out. "I like nice food and wine, and if I'm house poor, then I can't afford good food."

"I'll take care of the food," he insisted.

"I just—"

"How about we look at it on Friday, after you meet with Devlin. Kim can give you all of the information, *then* we'll go from there."

"I just don't want to waste anyone's time."

"You're not." He smiled. "Trust me."

"Fine," I breathed out. "We'll go look at what will probably be a dream place that I won't be able to afford."

"That's the spirit." He dragged me back onto his lap and kissed me.

"I'm gonna need to get home soon."

"Yeah. You wanna go now?"

"If it means we can make out a bit before you leave me, then, yes."

"Well, that's really up to you." He slid his hand to my neck. "I can stay all night if you want me to."

I closed my eyes briefly. "You're seriously going to make me lose my religion."

"One can hope."

I met his eyes. "Let's go now, but promise me you won't stay, even if I beg."

He raised an eyebrow. "Not gonna do that, baby. Because there's no way in hell I'll be able to resist you."

I wrinkled my nose. "It was worth a shot."

He kissed me again. "Let's grab our stuff."

I nodded and we headed out.

TWELVE

BURNING SAINTS

Trixie

SUNDAY MORNING, I was dragging. I'd obviously pushed my luck getting home so late, and then making out with Spike for close to an hour before he reluctantly left me.

I managed to make it down to the garage before my parents came looking for me (because, god forbid I drove myself), having managed to remember my Bible this time. I did not, however, have time for coffee, so I had to force myself not to yawn. The effort meant my eyes were watery and my nose was slightly runny.

My parents did not greet me, my mother gave me the once-over with her 'discerning' look, then slid into the front passenger seat just before I slid into the back.

I felt like I was crawling out of my skin as we pulled into the church parking lot, and I had a quick daydream of running away. I wondered how far I'd get in a skirt and wedges, but knew I was being overly dramatic... plus, I probably wouldn't even make it around the block before I dropped dead from the effort.

I followed behind my parents as we headed inside and I heard my mother hiss slightly under her breath, "What is *he* doing here?"

I followed her line of sight to see Spike leaning against the brick wall, his hand holding his cell phone, two cups of coffee in the other.

I let out an internal squeak and rushed past my parents to meet him. "What are you doing here?"

He grinned, sliding his phone into his pocket before handing me one of the coffees. "Well, I figured you came to my place last night, met my friends and family, it's only fair I come to you."

"But it's *church.*"

"Baby, I'd go to hell if it meant I was with you."

I bit my lip. "I want to kiss you so bad right now."

He chuckled. "Same."

My parents arrived and my father bristled as he reluctantly held his hand out to Spike. "Spike. Glad to see you at church. I hope the Lord speaks to you, *clearly*, this morning."

Spike shook his hand and nodded. "Looking forward to the spiritual enlightenment, *pastor.*"

I had to bite the inside of my cheek to keep from laughing.

My mother plastered a fake smile on her face and slid her hand into the crook of my father's arm. "We should get inside."

"We'll see you both in there," Daddy said, and led my mother away.

"Hi," I breathed out.

"Hey, baby." He glanced over my head, then leaned down to kiss me quickly. "How was your morning?"

"Good now." I held up my coffee. "How did you know I needed this?"

He tapped his temple. "I can read your mind."

I wrinkled my nose. "Well, that's terrifying."

He laughed. "Oh, I know."

"Last chance to save yourself."

"It's us against the world, baby." He held his hand out to me. "You with me?"

I linked my fingers with his and nodded. He raised our hands to his lips, kissing the back of mine before we headed inside.

I led him down the aisle to our family pew only to find my mother had blocked off the seats beside her with programs. "There's just no room for him to sit here," she said.

"Then I'm not either."

"Don't be dramatic, Christine."

I scowled at her and walked Spike to the back of the church. I refused to sit anywhere near her.

"Baller move, baby," Spike whispered as we took our seats.

The band took the stage and we were instructed to stand, so we did. For the next hour and fifteen minutes, Spike was the perfect congregant as the service dragged on.

Me, not so much.

I wanted out, so the second we were dismissed, I grabbed Spike's hand, and pulled him out the side door. "Please tell me you brought your bike."

"I did not."

I frowned. "What? Why not?"

"Because I brought one of the trucks."

"Oh," I squeaked. "Do you have to have it back soon?"

"No."

"Are you trying to annoy me right now?"

He chuckled. "Just a little bit."

"Take me away from here," I demanded. "I want out."

"Hold that thought." He slid his phone from his pocket. "Hello? Yeah, it's Spike. Oh, hey, Kim. Oh, yeah? Sure." He met my eyes. "Want to go see her place after lunch?"

"I can't afford—"

"Yeah, we'll be there. Thanks, sweetheart." He hung up and slid his phone back in his pocket. "Where do you want to eat?"

"Spike."

"Right here, beautiful."

I glared up at him. "Oh, never mind."

"Wise choice."

"I want Italian."

"Great, I know just the place."

"Fantastic," I hissed.

Spike laughed, leaning down to kiss me before leading me to the truck.

* * *

"I have to take a call," Kim said. "I'll give you some time to look around. Text me when you're ready."

"Thanks," Spike said, and walked her to the door.

Once he closed and locked it, I threw my hands in the air. "There's no way."

"She told you the rent."

"There's no way she can even keep the lights on charging me that little." I walked to the living room windows that overlooked the Willamette River. Oh my word, the view was to die for. The condo had two bedrooms, two bathrooms, a large kitchen with a giant island and great room, plus an office. It had just been updated, but Kim had kept its old-world style and it was gorgeous.

Spike's hands came around my waist and he kissed the back of my neck. "I could fuck you up against these windows and no one would see."

I shivered. "Spike, stop."

"You're gonna take this place, baby, and you're gonna trust that my people won't fuck you over."

"It's too good to be true." I faced him. "*You're* too good to be true."

"We'll make it work, baby."

I grimaced. "Well, let's get me a job before I commit to anything, okay?"

"I will cover the rent until you find something, honey. It's more important that you get out from under your parents' roof."

"I don't feel comfortable with you paying my rent, Spike."

"We can talk about that later. I'll let Kim know you're taking the place."

"Jesse," I hissed.

"Right here, baby."

"Oh, never mind."

He dropped his head back and muttered to the ceiling, "She's learning."

"Don't be ornery," I ordered, and he laughed before kissing me quickly.

Spike texted Kim, then we headed out to the truck.

* * *

Jenson and I decided to meet for lunch on Monday instead of dinner since we both had time. It meant I could talk to him about the job in a more relaxed environment, and he didn't feel like he needed to pick me up (he had this weird thing about me not driving at night).

I pulled up to our favorite taco truck downtown just after eleven and found him already sitting at a picnic table under a giant umbrella. He had his head buried in his phone and he was frowning. I took a second to watch him, but the second he saw me, he grinned, rising to his feet and pulling me in for a hug. "Hey, sissy."

"Hey, are you okay?"

"A chance to have uninterrupted time with my favorite sister? I'm fuckin' great. Are you okay?"

I chuckled. "Yes, I'm great. Did you order?"

"Nope." He grinned. "Waiting for you."

We took a few minutes to order, grab napkins and utensils, then headed back to the table.

"I need to talk to you about something."

"Uh-oh, that sounds ominous."

"No, it's a good thing... I hope."

He settled his elbows on the table and studied me. "Give it to me."

"Devlin's offered me a job."

"Oh yeah?"

I nodded. "Office manager, receptionist, etcetera."

He cocked his head. "You'd be perfect for that."

I narrowed my eyes. "But I'd be all up in your grill."

He frowned. "Why would I give one fuck about that?"

I shrugged. "Because I'm your little sister and I don't want to be the *annoying* little sister."

"Jesus, Christine, that's Mom talking, not me. I adore your face, and you know it. I would love to see you every day."

"I just don't want to cramp your style."

He smiled. "You couldn't if you tried."

"Are you sure?"

"Hell, yeah."

I sighed. "Okay, I'll do the interview, then."

"Sissy, you seriously need to not worry about what other people think. You're awesome just the way you are."

I blushed. "That's what Spike says."

"Tell me more about this guy. Who is he?"

"You met him, what do you think?"

He shook his head. "The Saints aren't guys you fuck with, Chrissy. How did you meet a fuckin' biker? Jesus, you don't run in the same circles."

"Why do I feel like I'm getting grilled, Jens?" I raised an eyebrow. "Which is it? Am I supposed to not worry about what other people think, or just worry about what *you* think?"

He sighed. "You're right. I'm sorry. I just want you safe."

"I get it. And I met Spike in high school. You know that picture you drew of me? The one where I was really sad?"

Jenson nodded.

"I'd met him that night and Mom was really nasty to him. We connected, but then he went back to prison and I went back to church."

"And what's with the Trixie thing?"

"He misheard my name and I didn't correct him because I thought it was sweet. I guess he'd tried to find me when he got out, so when we ran into each other outside of Devlin's shop, it was kind of a miracle."

He tapped his fingers on the table as he contemplated my words. "So what's the plan here, sissy?"

"I love him, Jens."

His eyes widened. "You've just met the guy."

Before I could respond, our order number was called, so Jenson retrieved our food and drinks, then sat down again.

"I haven't just met him, big brother. We met a long time ago, and reconnected. I know him."

"You *don't* know him. You met him once, then met him again. He's an ex-con, Chrissy."

"He didn't do anything wrong, Jenson. He was a kid and he was railroaded." I cringed internally at my unintentional pun.

"Every criminal says they're innocent," he muttered.

"Oh my word, I'm done," I bit out. "I'm not sitting here and listening to you talk about him that way. You need to get to know him so you make your own decision, because I think you'll find you'll like him, but if you don't, you need to keep your mouth shut because I love him, and he's not going anywhere."

"When did you get a backbone?"

"About five minutes ago."

My brother chuckled. "I'll give him a chance, sissy. But if he breaks your heart, I'm gonna break his kneecaps."

I sighed. "I can live with that."

"Eat," he ordered, and I mean mugged him before diving in.

We spent the next half-hour catching up but he still didn't give me any useful information. My brother had always been discreet, but for the last few years he was what you would call 'closed off.' A vault, if you will.

Not that he was a sharer. Matty was the chatty one and if I was going to tell my secrets to anyone, it would be Mattias. I just assumed it went the same way with Jenson. But now I wondered if maybe he was just as monosyllabic with Mattias as he was being with me.

I decided to drop it for the moment, mostly because I didn't want to be a hypocrite and meddle in his business when I'd just asked him to keep his nose out of mine, but

I loved him and I couldn't stop myself from worrying, all the same.

Jenson had a client, so he walked me to my car and I headed home, pulling into the garage just as Spike called.

"Hi there, handsome."

"Oooh, I like that," he said with a laugh.

"Good to know." I grinned, turning off my car.

"You busy tonight?"

"No, why?"

"You wanna come see the club?" he asked.

"Yes, please."

"Okay, I'll pick you up at six. We'll eat there."

"Okay, see you then."

"We'll be on my bike, so dress warm."

"Yes, sir," I retorted.

Spike laughed. "Like that too, baby."

"I'll keep that in mind."

We rang off and I headed inside to change.

* * *

Spike picked me up a little early but stopped me just before we reached his bike.

"Wait here and close your eyes," he said, blocking my view with his gorgeous body.

"What is this?"

"Just close your eyes and wait here," he ordered, leaving me just at the bottom of my stairs.

I did as Spike instructed, closing my eyes, and fighting the urge to peek.

"Okay," Spike said. "You can look now."

I opened my eyes to see Spike holding a sparkly, blue motorcycle helmet, topped with a big red bow.

"For me?" I asked, shocked by the gift.

"It's got your name on it, doesn't it?" Spike turned the

helmet around to reveal 'Trixie' monogramed on the back. "Try it on."

"I can't believe you got me this," I said, kissing him. "It's beautiful."

"Not as beautiful as the head it's gonna protect. Besides, now you don't have to wear mine."

I chuckled. "Should I keep the bow on top?"

"Probably not," he replied with a grin. "People might mistake you for a motorcycle cop."

"I love it." I pulled his head down for another kiss.

"Oh, I almost forgot the best part. Check it out," he said, excitedly, pointing to the inside of the helmet. "Both of our helmets are equipped with mics and speaker, connected via Blue Tooth. We can talk to each other or share a playlist while were riding."

"It's perfect," I said, slipping the helmet on, before climbing onto the back of Spike's bike.

He started the engine and my stomach fluttered in anticipation of what was to come. I loved riding with Spike more than I could have possibly predicted. Before Spike, I'd never given much thought to motorcycles one way or another. I certainly never imagined what it might be like to be on one. Not that my imagination would have compared to the real thing. My arms wrapped around Spike, while my legs straddled the bike. According to Spike, the engine was a V-Twin and produced an average of one hundred horsepower. All I knew was the roar of the engine, and the vibrations it sent through my body were exhilarating. It also made me very *horny*, which was a word I didn't ever expect to use when referring to myself, but there it was.

As we drove through the rapidly changing landscape of Portland, I felt as though I was seeing the city for the first time. Being with Spike was like putting on a pair of magic glasses that allowed me to see things that were otherwise hidden to me. I saw both the beauty and sadness of the city and its people with far more clarity and empathy.

My whole life, I'd been forced to view the world through my father's interpretation of God's lens. A lens that revealed every good thing was of God, and every bad thing was of Satan, done with the hands of mankind. Maybe my father was right and the world was just that cut and dry, but I didn't feel that way when I was with Spike. When I looked at him, I saw possibilities. Not of what he could become, but of what I could become. Spike showed me what it meant to be brave and rebellious. How to display righteous anger, but also have mercy on those who've harmed you in the past. He showed me what patience and unconditional love looked like. He was, simply put, the person who most exhibited the traits of Jesus more than anyone I'd ever met.

But Jesus never made me horny, and the more I was around Spike, the more I wanted him to do things to me. Things I'd never wanted a man to do to me before.

Driving through an area of town I never even knew existed, we stopped at a large gate with a guard tower. The guard posted in the tower gave Spike a chin lift before opening the entrance and allowing us access.

"Why the security?" I asked.

"Better safe than sorry," Spike replied.

"That setup looked a little more serious than basic safety precautions."

"Since going legitimate, the club has faced some challenges."

"Which is code for…?"

Spike sighed. "Look, I can't give you details, but I will say we've faced the kind of challenges that make everyone feel a whole lot better with a gate and guards posted at all times."

Spike stopped and parked his bike near what looked like a hunting lodge. We climbed off and removed our helmets.

I bit my lip. "Am I safe here?"

Spike pulled me close. "I would have never brought you here if it meant putting you in danger. In fact, this is probably the safest place in Portland. I'd rather you be here with me than anywhere else. Besides, you should feel right at home at a place called the 'Sanctuary.'"

"I suppose I am in the company of saints, aren't I?"

"Don't let the halos fool you, baby. My brothers play on the squeaky side, but they are far from clean. You understand?"

I nodded. What I really understood was how my body reacted when he called me 'baby.'

Is this what being in heat feels like?

"Let's go inside, so I can show you off," he said, opening and holding the door for me.

The Sanctuary, Spike had explained, was a compound made up of multiple buildings, including bunk houses, workshops, garage bays, and whatever else the club needed, including its very own, newly built tavern, 'Warthog's Watering Hole,' named after one of the club's oldest members.

"The Bar is kinda like Warthog's retirement fund," Spike said as we made our way inside. "He's always been the club's unofficial bartender, so he may as well make a few bucks while he's at it."

"This place is beautiful," I breathed, surprised by what I saw once inside. The Sanctuary's main building, called the Chapel, was decorated like an Adirondack hunting lodge from the turn of the century.

Spike motioned to the various trophies adorning the space. "All these antlers and animal hides are from game bagged by Cutter, and a couple of the old timers."

"What? They didn't want to stuff 'em and prop them up in the corners?"

"These skins and antlers are all that are left," Spike said. "Cutter believed hunters should show the same amount of respect and reverence for their prey this country's native people showed. They wasted nothing. Some even made kuttes from deer and elk hides."

"I thought I heard the sound of a beautiful woman coming from in here," Clutch said as he entered the room.

"Hi," I said, greeting him with a hug." I'd met Clutch and his wife at the Dogs' clubhouse and he had a very intense look about him but there was an inner sweetness that couldn't help but shine through him, and his wife was a total rock star. I hoped to get to know them both more, which of course meant I was hoping to be around Spike for as long as possible, but I was trying hard not to get my hopes up. Half expecting him to dump me once he figured out how boring I was.

Clutch punched Spike in the arm. "This guy treating you with respect?"

"So far," I replied.

"Yeah, well, if that changes you let me know. My wife, quote-unquote, adores you, and I'll be forced to tar and feather him, if he fucks up."

"You'll be the first to know," I assured him.

"Anyone else around?" Spike asked.

"It's been pretty quiet here all day. Minus sent some guys on a run, a few others are in the shop, and the Prez is with Cricket down at city hall, fighting with the zoning commission over the skate park."

My eyebrows shot up. "You guys are building a skate park?"

"It's not for us," Clutch said.

"Speak for yourself, old man," Spike said.

Clutch punched Spike's arm again. Audibly harder

this time.

Spike winced and smiled.

"It's for the neighborhood kids," Clutch said. "Two parks in Portland have closed down over the past year and the locals are running out of places to skate."

"Why build another park if others are closing?" I asked.

"They're closing because they haven't been able to figure out how to turn a constant profit, plus cover the insurance costs. We don't have to worry so much about that. In fact, we could lose money and it would still be a great tax write off."

Spike nodded. "Not to mention, the good it will spread within the community."

"If we can ever get the zoning commissioner to sign off on our plans," Clutch said. "Until then, the whole project is dead in the water."

"My father probably plays golf with the commissioner," I said. "I wonder if there is some way I could convince him to put in a good word for the club."

"And in other news," Spike said in an announcer voice. "Recent studies have shown that due to climate change, the temperature in hell is decreasing rapidly."

I smacked his chest playfully. Although, he was probably right. My father would more than likely be the last person who would want to help the club.

"It's good to see you again, babe," Clutch said, kissing my cheek. "I've gotta go pick up eyedrops for the kid, and then I've got a hot date with my wife and her fine ass."

"See you 'round," Spike said, giving Clutch a chin lift as he made his exit. He then turned to me. "C'mon. There's someplace special I want to show you."

"What is it?" I asked.

"It's a surprise."

"You should know I hate surprises," I said. "I peeked at my Christmas presents under the tree every year, and I read the last page of every book, before I start it."

Spike furrowed his brow. "War crimes. You should be brought up on war crimes.

He took me by the hand and led me back outside, through the center of the complex, out towards a medium-sized, standalone building, that stood about fifty yards away from anything else.

"What is this?" I asked.

Spike produced a key from his pocket and gave me a nervous looking smile. "I've never shown anyone my place before."

"This is where you live?"

Spike nodded. "Although, truth be told. I do more working here than living."

He unlocked the door and ushered me inside to reveal a large, open workspace, littered with carts, tools, and bins full of scrap metal and junk. In one corner of the room was a box spring and mattress, and next to it, an orange crate being used as a nightstand. There was also a mini fridge and a hotplate, completing the total amount of domestic items found within the space.

All of that may sound horrible, and believe me it was, but in stark contrast of the living conditions were the beautiful sculptures found throughout the place. At least a dozen of them. Bold, metallic, abstract, works that were unlike anything I'd ever seen.

"Did you make these?" I whispered.

Spike smiled. "Do you like them?"

"They're stunning," I replied, studying each piece.

"Why are you whispering?"

I laughed. "I don't know. They're all just so beautiful, I feel like I'm in a museum or something."

"Thank you, but I doubt my work would ever be

featured in a museum or gallery."

"Why not?"

"First of all, I'd have to be a great sculptor for anyone to take notice, and I'm not great, I'm just...me. And, secondly, I'd have to show my work to another living soul. Besides you, of course."

I was stunned. "You've never shown these to anyone?"

He shook his head. "You're the first."

"What about your teachers?"

"Self-taught. Just like everything else. Once I figured out how to weld, my mind began to flood with ideas. I searched the internet for anything I could find on the subject as well as studying the works of the modern masters, Ai Weiwei, Louise Bourgeois, and Antony Gormley."

"Spike, that's incredible. These are amazing. I can't believe you're sharing them with me."

"You really like my stuff?"

"I love them. Especially this one," I said, pointing to the piece at the center of the room.

The sculpture was around eight feet tall and appeared to be made entirely from pieces of rusted metal. The various shades of oxidized red metal, formed into the flames that danced around the wire frame of a woman, reaching upwards to a cluster of stars which hung high over her head.

"It's based on Joan of Arc," Spike said.

"It's so beautiful it makes me want to cry."

"It's for you," he said, taking my hands in his.

"What?"

"I started it the night after we met again at Devlin's shop, and I finished last night. Here. Take a look," he said, showing me an engraved plaque attached to the bottom of the sculpture which read, "For Trixie. Too busy reaching for heaven to be touched by the flames of hell."

I burst into tears and dropped my head to his chest as I wrapped my arms around his waist. "Spike."

"Oh, honey, I didn't mean to make you cry."

"It's just, so... beautiful."

"You're beautiful." He lifted my chin. "I need to taste you or I'm gonna go crazy."

I licked my lips. "I don't know what that means."

He slid his hand between my legs.

"Oh," I squeaked as he knelt in front of me and pressed his face to apex of my thighs. "Spike," I whispered, sliding my fingers into his hair.

"Tell me this is okay," he begged.

I swallowed. "What about... hell?"

He looked up at me and gripped the outside of my thighs. "You won't go to hell, baby. Swear."

I dropped my head back again and admitted, "Well, I'm at the point that I'm not sure if I care."

Spike slid my jeans and panties down my thighs, pressing his mouth to my mound and I mewed as his tongue stroked my clit. I cried out at the sensations swamping me.

"I'm gonna fall," I panted.

Spike stood, picking me up with ease and carrying me to the mattress, laying me gently on top.

"If you want me to stop, tell me," Spike said.

I squeezed my eyes shut. "I don't want you to stop."

He kneeled between my legs again, guiding one of them over his shoulder before settling his mouth over my core. I arched into him as I fisted my hands into the sheets and he licked, sucked, and ate his way around my nether regions.

I'd never experienced anything like it before.

When he slid a finger inside of me, however, I could no longer hold back my reaction, and I cried out as my body shuddered with release.

I let go of the bedding and took several deep breaths as I came down from my orgasmic high, and Spike kissed the inside of each thigh, snagging my panties off the floor and handing them back to me. "I knew you'd taste like that."

I pulled on my underwear and asked, "Like what?"

He slid his finger (the one that had just been inside of me) into his mouth and sucked it clean. "Vanilla."

I blushed and covered my face with my hands. "Oh my word, stop."

He chuckled, gently pulling my hands down. "How ya doin'?"

I bit my lip. "I'm fine."

"You sure?"

I nodded. "That was... well, amazing. I've never felt like that before."

"Have you never done that to yourself?"

"I'm not that flexible," I retorted, and he laughed.

"That's not what I meant and you know it."

I sighed. "No, I can't say that I have done that before. It has been drilled into me that sex, of any kind, is a sin and a direct link to hell."

"Well, that's just sad."

"Yes, it really is because that was beyond nice."

He smiled. "Fuck, yeah, it was."

"I hope we can do that again."

"Abso-fucking-lutely. You just say the word."

I smiled. "The word."

He laughed, and his face was suddenly buried between my legs again.

THIRTEEN

Trixie

WEDNESDAY MORNING, I drove down to Devlin's shop, ridiculously early for my interview. I had just parked my car when my phone rang. Seeing it was Spike, I answered. "Hey, honey."

"Jesus, I don't know what I like better."

"What do you mean?"

"You callin' me Jesse or honey."

"Really?" I smiled. "How do you feel about pookie bear?"

"Let's put a pin in that one."

"Kinky."

He chuckled. "You ready for your meeting?"

"Not at all," I breathed out. "I'm already here, which just proves how much of a nerd I am."

"Baby, you're gonna do great. Why are you so nervous?"

"Because I'm this sheltered pastor's kid and y'all are these larger than life, seen and done almost everything, cool as heck—" I sighed. "I don't even know what I'm saying."

"I get it, baby, but you're cool, too, you know."

I dropped my head to the steering wheel. "No I'm not. I'm an anxiety ridden, insecure, and overweight woman who constantly questions her decisions, especially when she's about to walk into a tattoo shop and interview for a *job*."

A knock at my car window elicited a quiet squeak from me and I whipped my head up to see Spike leaning in with a frown.

I rolled the window down and hissed, "You scared me to death."

"If you call yourself overweight one more fuckin' time, I'm gonna lose my shit, woman. Got it?" He pulled open my door so he could get face-to-face with me. "You are beautiful and perfect and sexy. Not to mention, compassionate, generous, and, honestly, the kindest person I've ever met. Take it from the guy who fantasized about you for years, you're even better in real life."

I grabbed his face and kissed him, desperately wanting to take him somewhere private. It was him who broke the connection, dropping his forehead to mine before unbuckling my seatbelt and stepping back. "Jesus."

"Sorry." I grimaced. "I didn't expect that to be so... intense."

He raised an eyebrow. "Baby, you've kissed me

before, it's always intense."

I sighed. "Point taken."

He chuckled. "Come on, I'll walk you in."

"Ah, no, you won't."

"Why not?"

I grabbed my purse and stepped out of my car, rolling up my window before closing my door. "Because my boyfriend is not babysitting me during my interview."

"I'm not babysitting you. I happen to be working here today."

I cocked my head. "And did you work your schedule around my interview so you could be here in case I needed emotional support?"

He studied me for a few seconds before muttering, "I plead the fifth."

"Do not walk in with me"—I tugged on his jacket—"And I don't want to see you until I text you and tell you I'm done with the interview. Then we'll meet outside and maybe you can walk me back to my car. Got it?"

"No, that won't work."

"Why not?"

"Because I'm taking you to lunch or brunch, or whatever when you're done."

"I thought you said you had to work."

"My schedule's flexible."

I narrowed my eyes and let out a groan. "Flexible my butt. You're totally here to babysit me."

"Potato, tomato, either way you're gonna knock Devlin dead during this interview."

"Well, I don't want her dead, then who will pay me?"

"See? You've already got a dark, edgy sense of humor," he retorted. "You were *made* for a tattoo shop."

I rolled my eyes. "Do not interfere."

He raised his hands in surrender. "You won't even know I'm here."

I swung my purse over my shoulder and headed inside, finding Devlin at the front desk, the reception phone to her ear. Her face lit up when she saw me and she waved me over. "No, Jim, I told you, I have a client. I get it, but it doesn't matter, you can't just throw money at me like that. I don't bail on my clients. Two months and only because I had a cancelation." She rolled her eyes as she scribbled on a post-it. "Sure. Yep. Otherwise, you'll need to wait until June. No, I'm not kidding. Take it or wait. Good choice. I'll see you in two months. Bye." She hung up and faced me, sitting on the edge of the desk. "Good morning."

"Hi," I said. "Are you even open yet?"

"No, but Jim doesn't have my cell phone, for very good reason, and I saw his name pop up on the screen. I figured I'd save you the headache."

I chuckled. "I haven't even interviewed yet. You don't know if you're going to hire me."

"Oh, I'm hiring you." She handed me a stack of paperwork. "Here's your offer, insurance information, paid time off, etcetera. I just need you to sign it. But I'll show you around and give you a rundown of the job first, then you can figure out whether or not you want it."

"I'm more concerned about if I'm a right fit for you, to be honest. I love being an admin. I'm just, well, not the most experienced, and I've never worked in a tattoo shop before."

"I hire for attitude. The only place I care about skill is with my artists, but in my front desk and intern roles, I need people who are friendly and quick to learn, which I believe you are. The rest will work itself out." She grinned. "What I really need is someone who isn't full of crap and won't take crap, and considering the fact you're with Spike, I'm pretty sure you've got both covered."

"Are you really this cool?" I asked, then grimaced.

"Sorry, that was supposed to be my inside voice."

Devlin laughed. "Come on, let me show you around."

For the next hour, Devlin gave me a tour of the shop and with every passing moment, I felt like she was showing me my dream job. It was like it had been handpicked for me.

"So, what do you think?" she asked once we were back at the front desk.

"Everything sounds really great," I said.

"Awesome. I want you to take the day, look over the paperwork, then let me know what you think. You can start as early as tomorrow, if you like."

"Wow, okay, that's amazing, thank you."

"Now, I know there's a certain someone dying to take you to brunch, so I'll let him do that," she said.

I bit my lip. "Is he going to be a problem if I do take this job?"

"Not even a little bit." She scoffed. "Are you kidding me? Ropes is way into all kinds of PDA, and this"— she pointed to her expanding belly—"happened in my office just after we closed. As long as you get your work done and keep things professional in front of clients, I don't care what you do with your time. Within reason of course."

I blushed. "Sounds good."

She grinned and headed back behind the curtain as I texted Spike then gathered up the paperwork.

He came flying through the drapes with flourish and grinned. "When do you start?"

I chuckled. "I have to read through the paperwork, then make my decision."

"Great. You can do that while we eat. Give me your keys."

"My keys, why?"

"Because I had to haul shit in one of the big trucks, so

we're gonna take your car."

"Okay, so I'll drive."

He smirked. "Ah, no, I drive when we're together, baby."

"What kind of chauvinistic, misogynistic—"

"Not playin' that game, Trixie. You were born to be driven, so I'm drivin' you." He held his palm out to me and flapped it.

"I'm not Miss Daisy."

He cocked his head. "You saw Driving Miss Daisy?"

"Yes. In my social studies class. My father flipped his lid." She smiled. "I loved it."

"Did you love it more because your dad flipped his lid?"

"I plead the fifth."

Spike laughed and I reluctantly handed him my keys and led him out the front door.

* * *

"Spike?" I whispered.

"Yeah, baby?" he whispered back with a grin.

"Devlin's offering me twenty-grand more than I was making at my last job, plus five weeks paid time off, plus two weeks sick leave, and full medical and dental benefits. She also closes the shop over Christmas and that time's paid as well. So, that's like almost seven weeks off a year. How is this even possible?"

We were sitting in his favorite breakfast place on Mississippi, eating what I'd deemed the best French toast on the planet, and I was reading through the offer paperwork.

"She wants her people to feel taken care of so they don't leave," he said.

"It's too good to be true."

"We take care of our own, Trixie," he said and took a

sip of his coffee.

"I don't know if I can live up to this, though."

He frowned, setting his mug on the table. "What the fuck did your parents do to you?"

"I don't know that I can blame my parents for everything, honey. I'm inexperienced."

"And she said she hires for attitude, right? You have a great attitude. She'll train you for all the other stuff." He reached over and squeezed my hand. "Give yourself a break and take the chance."

I bit my lip. "It does mean I might actually be able to afford Kim's place."

"Good because you're moving in on Saturday."

I gasped. "What?"

"Already set it up. It comes mostly furnished other than the bed."

"All I have is my bed and my cuddle chair. I mean, other than clothes and a few personal things."

"Easy move then. I'll come by on Saturday morning and help you load up."

"What about the deposit? I need to send that to her."

"Already done."

I narrowed my eyes at him. "And how much was that?"

"Not telling you."

"Why not?"

"Because then you'll want to pay me back and that's not happenin'." He smiled. "Text Devlin and tell her you're taking the job. We'll move you into Kim's on Saturday and you can celebrate on Sunday by sleeping in."

I sighed, closing my eyes. "That sounds like a dream."

"Take a chance, baby."

I opened my eyes and smiled. "Okay."

He grinned. "Okay."

I texted Devlin, accepted the job, then we finished our

breakfast, and headed back to the shop.

* * *

Spike

We had just finished loading up the van with Trixie's belongings, and were ready to take off, when Gary's car pulled into the driveway. The Lincoln screeched to a halt before Gary spilled out of the driver's seat onto the concrete. He was bloodied and bruised, and his shirt was torn near the collar. I'd seen enough guys take a beating in my life to know that someone had worked the good pastor over, big time.

I handed Tacky Trixie's keys so he could drive her car to the new place. I wanted her with me because I had a feeling she was going to need to process whatever the fuck was going on and I didn't want her driving while she did it.

"Oh, my word, Daddy!" Trixie cried, running to her father, me right behind.

"I'm alright, I'm alright," he said, rising unsteadily to his feet. "I just slipped getting out of the car, that's all."

"You're all bloody. What happened?"

"Oh, it's nothing," Gary said, waving his daughter off. "I was alone at the church and noticed that a light had gone out in the foyer. I decided I'd change it myself because I knew I wouldn't remember to tell Carl on Sunday. Anyway, I got a ladder from the supply closet and climbed up with a fresh bulb and must have lost my balance."

"Daddy, you could have broken your neck," Trixie said, examining her father.

I didn't know why Gary was lying, but I had a suspicion that it had something to do with the white powder I'd spied earlier in his moustache.

"Why didn't you call 9-1-1? Or drive to the hospital? You could have a concussion, or internal injuries."

"Don't be silly, pumpkin, I'm fine. I just need one of my back pills, and a soak in a hot bath."

Back pills, my ass.

We helped him inside where Sherri took over.

"What were you thinking, going up on a ladder like that?" she admonished as she helped him up the stairs.

As soon as her parents were out of earshot, I turned to Trixie. "We need to talk about your father."

"He may not be president of your fan club now, but I know once he gets to know you more, he'll—"

"No, it's not about me and him, it's about the bruises and the blood."

"The accident?"

I shook my head. "Your father didn't fall off a ladder."

She frowned. "What? How do you know?"

"The bruises on his face and neck are from a beating."

Her face scrunched up in horror. "You're saying someone beat my father up? Who would do that and why would he lie to me about it? Do you think someone at the church did this and he's covering for them?

"It could be, but I don't think so," I said.

"Why don't you think so?"

"There's something else I have to tell you."

"What is it?"

I scrubbed the back of my neck. "The other night when your dad invited me into his study, he excused himself to go to the bathroom and when he came out, I saw white powder in his moustache?"

"White powder?" She cocked her head. "What, like cocaine? Are you saying my dad does cocaine?"

"I don't know. It could have been. Or maybe it was crushed up pills. A lot of people get strung out on pain medication." I met her eyes. "When did he hurt his back?"

"I don't know." She shrugged. "Maybe five or six years ago."

"Do you know what kind of medicine he was prescribed?"

She shook her head.

"It's not just the powder, either. When he came back from the can, he was agitated, sweating and his pupils were like pinpoints. I've seen enough guys on opioids to know the signs and I've seen enough fights to know when a man's been beaten by another man." I took Trixie's hands in mine. "Baby, I think your dad is in some serious trouble."

FOURTEEN

BURNING SAINTS

Trixie

WHATEVER SPIKE SAID next was drowned out by the sound of bees swarming inside my head as my field of vision narrowed and I felt lightheaded.

"I think I'm gonna pass out," I said, reaching for him before everything went black.

The next thing I remember was the sensation of lying on grass, triggering happy childhood memories of running through the sprinklers with my brothers.

"Trixie, Trixie!" they called to me as we jumped over

the oscillating streams of water. "Trixie, can you hear me?" Mattias asked, but it wasn't his voice.

It was... Spike's? Why was I running through the sprinklers with Spike?

My eyelids fluttered open to reveal him standing over me.

"There you are," he said with a smile.

"What happened?" I asked, attempting to sit up.

"Hold on," Spike said, gently. "Let's just take our time getting up. You passed out for a few tics, but I caught you."

"Thank you."

Spike frowned. "This kind of thing happen to you often?"

"I'm not sure often is the right word." I shook my head. "It hasn't happened for a long time. Not since I was thirteen and fainted at Wendy Carmichael's birthday sleepover."

"Lemme guess. A couple of sips of Boones Farm and you were out cold?"

"What's Boones Farm?"

"The cheapest wine on the market."

"Oh, ah, no, worse. Since Wendy was turning thirteen, her mom allowed her to rent her first PG-13 movie." I shuddered. "She chose Insidious."

"The one about the possessed little boy?"

I shrugged. "I wouldn't know. I'd never seen a horror movie before and I was so scared, I passed out during the opening credits. Everyone was freaking out, and my dad had to come pick me up early. I was so mortified. It was the most embarrassing thing ever."

"Why were you embarrassed? You didn't do anything to feel ashamed of," Spike said.

I narrowed my eyes at him. "I'm going to assume you've never been a thirteen-year-old girl."

155

He smiled gently. "I've been many things during my short time on earth, but that's definitely not one of them."

"Well, I was, and I'll tell you something. I'd pit a gang of vicious eighth grade girls against the Burning Saints any day. Tween and teen girls pounce on the smell of a single drop of blood. Show any weakness and you're dead before you know it. Or even worse, ostracized by your peers. Banished to the land of the uncool and unpopular."

Spike chuckled. "Sounds a lot like prison."

"There were times during my teenage years I probably would have traded places with you."

Spike smiled in a way that said I was likely wrong in thinking that, before asking, "Did anyone ever figure out what was causing your fainting spells?"

"My parents took me to every medical doctor and faith healer they could, until finally resorting to a child psychologist."

Spike's face twisted up in question. "Resorting to? Why the hesitation?"

"My father has little love for mental health professionals. He believes, firmly, that most matters of the mind should be addressed from a spiritual perspective rather than a medical one. He felt my fainting spells were the result of a spiritual attack. Proved all the more to him when I fainted while watching a 'demonic' movie."

"What did your psychologist say?"

"That there was nothing wrong with me, and that my passing out was simply due to a lack of oxygen going to my brain. A natural fear response is freezing up, and when I would get scared, I'd be so frozen I'd forget to breathe. So, Dr. Charmain, taught me a series of breathing exercises to practice and employ when feeling scared or anxious."

Spike grimaced. "Sorry, I didn't mean to spring the

stuff about your dad on you like that."

"It's not your fault." I squeezed Spike's hand. "I just can't believe he'd be mixed up with the kind of people that could do something like that to him."

"I think I should talk to him," he said.

"I'm not sure that's the best idea."

"He's not gonna be honest with you or your mother, but if I can handle this right, I think he'll be straight with me." Spike met my eyes. "If he is, I might be able to help him."

"And if he's not straight with you?"

"Then I'm all the happier that you're not living here anymore."

"Why?"

"Because whoever worked your father over won't have any problem hurting you or your mother if your pops doesn't make things right with them."

"I can't leave my mom here alone if she's in danger."

"You're not going to. I'll talk to Minus about posting some brothers to stand guard over this place. But for now, I need to talk to your dad... alone."

* * *

Spike

I walked Trixie back inside and got her settled on the couch before making my way upstairs to her parents' room. I knocked on the bedroom door and Sherri Mitchell answered.

"Yes, what is it?" she asked, her face framed in between the door and the jamb.

"I need to talk with Gary," I said.

"Pastor is resting in bed right now. Whatever it is you need to talk with him about is going to have to wait until later."

157

Sherri attempted to close the door, but my boot stopped it.

"Later is no good for me," I said, pushing my way into the room.

Gary sat up and shouted, "Get out of this room and out of this house, right now!"

I motioned to the cuts and bruises on his face. "You wanna talk about this in front of her or in private?"

"I don't have anything to say to you, at all. Sherri, call the police."

Sherri picked up the phone from the night stand next to Gary.

I threw my hands in the air. "Okay, have it your way. Tell me, then. Who does your dealer work for? Los Psychos? The Spiders?"

"What is he talking about?" Sherri asked.

"I have no idea," Gary sputtered out. "This man's crazy."

"Your family is in danger," I warned her, turning back to Gary. "But if you talk to me, I can help you."

"I don't need help from you," Gary seethed.

I motioned to the phone in Sherri's hands. "Go ahead, call the police. Tell 'em your husband was beat up by thugs, likely over an unpaid debt for dope. Watch how long it takes 'em to get here."

"What is he talking about, Gary?" Sherri said, hanging up the phone.

"I have no idea," Gary said.

"He didn't get those bruises falling off a ladder, Mrs. Mitchell," I said. "You're a smart woman, you can see that."

Gary rose to his feet. "You leave my wife out of this."

I crossed my arms and scowled. "The drug dealers you owe will do even worse to your family if you don't let me help you."

"He's telling the truth, isn't he?" Sherri asked her husband.

Gary scoffed. "I can't believe you're listening to this... this... hoodlum."

"Your mood swings, the secrecy." She threw her arms in the air. "I thought maybe you were having an affair, but this makes sense. I knew you'd sometimes take an extra pill without telling me, but I guess I figured you were in pain and didn't want to tell me."

Gary sat back down on the bed.

"It's way worse than sneaking a few pills, isn't it?" I asked.

He nodded.

"How bad are we talking?"

"It started when I hurt my back." Gary settled his hands on his knees. "The resort doctor wrote me up a three-month prescription of Vicodin. My back pain only lasted three weeks, but I kept on taking the pills. At first, I felt like God had gifted me with a second lease on life. The pills allowed me to preach for longer periods of time and with more vigor than I'd had in years. My knees no longer ached, I slept better, and I was in a better mood. Until I wasn't."

"Lemme guess. The party was over at the three-month mark?" I asked.

"The prescription was for three months." He grimaced. "I ran out after two. I was doubling up on most doses by then, and the pharmacy refused to refill the prescription without a new script from my stateside doctor. I was sick as a dog and crawling out of my skin, so I reached out to my doctor in Mexico, and he gave me the name of someone in Portland who could help me."

"Was then when you had that terrible flu?" Sherri asked.

"He was dope sick. Going through withdrawals," I

said.

"It was the worst I'd ever felt in my entire life," he admitted. "And I've had both malaria and Dengue fever."

"This guy in Portland. I assume he wasn't a doctor," I said.

Gary shook his head. "He sold me one-hundred Oxy-Contin, and sixty Vicodin. I gave half of the Vicodin to Sherri, so she'd think she was monitoring my usage, but I had the rest of the stash to use at my disposal."

Sherri began to cry. "Oh, Gary, how could you?"

"I thought I could make that number of pills last for six months, maybe longer. It was all gone in two, and I was back at the antique shop before I knew it."

My blood ran cold. There was only one dealer who worked out of an antique store, and he was definitely someone whose debt you did not want to find yourself in.

"You owe money to Edison?" I asked.

Gary nodded.

"Shit."

Oleg Volkov was an antiques dealer who emigrated to the US from Russia in the nineties. He was known on the streets as Edison, due to the large display of old lamps and lighting fixtures in his shop window. Although his storefront looked like Christmas all year round, Edison would never be mistaken as Santa Claus. He was tall, wiry, and incredibly strong. His head was shaved clean, and all visible skin was covered in what looked like Russian prison ink. And if he snuck into your house with a baseball bat, it wasn't to place it under your tree, it was to break your kneecaps with. Edison, ran dope, women, and black-market athletic apparel, as well as the city's biggest loansharking business. In fact, Edison would have been shut down a long time ago if two judges, and the city planning commissioner weren't all regular clients of his.

Oleg Volkov was brutal, merciless, and never forgave a debt.

Ever.

"The story gets worse," he said.

"The only thing worse than owing Edison money, is not paying him when he comes to collect," I said.

"Who is this Edison person and why do you owe him money? And how were you spending all this money on drugs without my knowledge?" Sherri shrieked. "I take care of the household finances and would have noticed any withdrawals."

"You used your church's money, didn't you?" I asked. "That's the part of the story that's worse."

He nodded again, bursting into tears.

"How much?"

"It...it gets...worse," Gary said in between the sobs.

"You can save those tears for when you are begging for your congregation's forgiveness. Right now, I need you to tell me how deep you're in with Edison."

"A...almost five...five hundred thousand," he stammered.

Sherri sat down on the bed beside her husband.

I exhaled deeply. "You couldn't have possibly spent all of that on pills."

"It started with the pills," Gary said. "But, within a year, I owed more than I could cover, so I...I stole ten grand from the children's ministry fund. No one noticed, so in nine months, when I needed more money, I did it again."

"When did you start upping the amount?" I asked.

"A little over a year ago, Mark Newport, a fellow pastor and good friend of mine told me about some hot investor tips he had. Real insider trading kind of stuff. The only catch was, in order to buy enough shares to make money, I'd have to invest at least one hundred grand.

Well, I didn't have any extra money to invest, so I borrowed two hundred thousand from the new building fund, which was temporarily on hold anyway, and invested it."

"You lost all of that money?" Sherri asked.

"No," Gary said, excitedly. "The tip paid off and I more than doubled the investment. But, instead of just putting all the money back, including what I'd already taken, I invested everything again, expecting the same results as the last time."

"But this time your horse didn't come in?"

He shook his head. "No, so I borrowed from Edison to replace the church funds before anyone noticed, thinking I'd have six months to reinvest, and make the money back to repay Edison and still make a profit. Only, God turned his favor from me once more, and I lost it all when the market crashed last year."

"And now, Edison wants his money," I said.

"Plus, interest. He told me I've got one week to pay him in full or he's gonna cut both of my ears off."

"Edison doesn't bluff." I dragged my hands down my face. "He'll have your lobes on a chain hanging from his neck if you don't have his cash in seven days. Then he'll stop being polite and start getting nasty."

Gary met my eyes. "Can you help me?"

"Let's get something crystal fucking clear," I said. "I'm gonna do whatever I can to help you, but not for your sake. I don't want Edison anywhere near Trixie. I don't even want him to know she exists. But you've put her and the rest of your family in danger, and I am not about to let a single hair on your daughter's head be so much as out of place."

"What...what are you going to do?"

I shook my head. "You don't ask questions, you do what I say, when I say it. That goes for the both of you. If you want to keep your house from being burned down with you in it, you'll follow my command. Understand?"

Trixie's folks nodded in agreement.

"Good. Then, I want the both of you to lay low. Get a fill in pastor to sub for you over the next few weeks and stay home and out of sight."

Now all I had to do was figure out how I was going to get one of the city's most notorious gangsters to back down.

FIFTEEN

BURNING SAINTS

Trixie

"**H**E WHAT?" I screeched as Spike filled me in on what my father had confessed.

We were in one of the club vans, hurtling toward my new place, all of my worldly belongings stacked in the back, and Spike had just filled me in on everything that had gone down with my father.

"He's gonna be okay, baby. We're gonna sort it out."

I let out a frustrated growl. "I don't actually care if you do 'sort it out,' Spike. Right now, I'm so angry, I could cut someone. Him, preferably. Maybe my mother.

Tiny cuts all over their bodies, after which I squeeze lemon juice into each and every one of them."

He laugh-snorted and bit out, "Jesus."

"I can't believe he's been shoving the Bible and piousness down everyone's throat while robbing his congregation *blind*, and shoving god knows what up his nose," I snapped. "And you know my mother knew exactly what was going on."

"She says she didn't."

"Well, then you can add *lying* to her list of sins." I scowled. "The wife always knows, unless they choose to turn a blind eye, and if that's the case, then she can go jump in a lake."

He reached over and took my hand. "It's gonna be okay, honey."

"Yes, I know it's going to be okay, and you know why I know it's going to be okay?"

"Why?"

"Because I'm *done*. Done, done. Finished with their lies and shenanigans. I'm taking a stand and I'm going to figure out what religion or god or whatever means to me. I've tried to do that in the past, but it's always under the filter of their lens. Not anymore. I'm having my Rumspringa and they aren't invited."

Spike burst out laughing as he squeezed my hand. "What the fuck is a Rum spring A?"

I faced him. "It's the thing where Amish teens leave their homes for a time to figure out if they want to be Amish."

"But you're not Amish."

"I know I'm not Amish, Jesse," I hissed. "But there isn't a name for young Christians who want to figure out if they still want to be Christians, so I'm adopting it."

He grinned. "Fair enough."

I was still fuming when we pulled into the parking

garage and parked in the loading zone. My car was already in my reserved space, and several of the Burning Saints were standing around waiting for us to arrive. I hadn't had to lift a finger during this move, which was kind of amazing, and something I could definitely get used to.

"We'll get everything moved in, then I'll make you dinner and open a bottle of wine. I want you to relax tonight." He smiled. "In fact, I want you to spend the rest of the weekend relaxing. Monday's gonna come fast."

I'd decided to wait and start my job with Devlin until Monday so I could get moved in and settled, and with all the crap going on with my dad, I was glad I gave myself a buffer.

I nodded. "I'm just looking forward to soaking in that giant tub."

"I'm gonna leave before you do that."

"You're going to leave?" I frowned. "Why?"

"Because if I know you're naked and that close to me, I'm not sure I can handle it."

"Don't leave." I reached over and squeezed his arm. "I won't take a bath if it makes it so you'll stay."

"Fuck." He squeezed his eyes shut. I waited a few seconds until he opened his eyes and smiled. "I'll stay, but you're gonna take your bath. I'll deal."

"Will you stay the night?"

His body locked and it took another few seconds for him to relax. "Yeah, baby, I'll stay the night."

I clapped my hands and let out a quiet squeal of excitement. "Yay."

"Jesus," he breathed out.

"What?"

"If you smile like that when I say yes to shit, what's gonna happen when I say no?"

I shrugged, batting my eyelashes at him. "Don't say

no and you'll never have to find out."

He laughed, pushing open his door and jumping down before collecting me. We spent the next hour moving everything in. Correction, his brothers spent the next hour moving everything in while I sat on the sofa and watched the water.

* * *

"Baby?" Spike called through the bathroom door.

"Yeah?"

"You want more wine?"

I was currently submerged in a giant clawfoot tub in the newly renovated bathroom of Kim's... ah, *my...* condo and I'd been here for nearly twenty minutes. I never wanted to leave.

I glanced at my wine glass, the tiny little puddle of red liquid at the bottom indicating that I did, in fact, want more wine. "Yes, please," I called back.

"Pull the curtain closed and I'll bring you the bottle."

I bit my lip. Lordy, he was sweet. He'd fed me (steak, baked potato, and asparagus), then he'd poured me a glass of wine while the tub was filling before leaving me to soak and relax. I'd heard the water running in the kitchen so I deduced he'd done the dishes while I pruned, and I loved him for it.

Now he was offering to honor my privacy by allowing me to close the shower curtain before he came in to deliver me wine.

This man was perfect.

"Come on in," I said.

The door opened and he bit out, "Fuck me."

I craned my neck with a smile. "Oops."

"Not fair, Trix."

I rose to my feet, the wine obviously emboldening me, and I reached for a towel. "I'm done being pious, Spike.

Do you love me?"

"With every fiber of my being."

"I love you, too," I said, wrapping the towel around myself. "I'm ready."

Spike helped me out of the tub, then he slid his hand to my neck and pulled me in for a gentle kiss. "We're gonna go slow, baby, but if you want to stop at any time, you tell me and we'll stop."

"What if we're, like, in the middle?"

"Then we'll stop." He stroked my cheek. "At any point, if you feel pain or discomfort, you tell me, got it?"

I blushed and gave him a nod. "Got it."

Taking my hand, he led me into my bedroom, and closed the drapes before removing his kutte and shirt and closing the distance between us. I shivered as I settled my palm against his chest, running a finger between his pecs, tracing the tattoo of the Burning Saints logo with a sword through the skull. He was lithe and sinewy and so incredibly gorgeous.

"I have no idea what to do," I admitted. "I mean, I know what to do, technically, but I… oh, pooh, I don't know what the heck I'm saying."

Spike cupped my face and smiled. "Baby, you're fine. I know what to do and you're just gonna follow my lead. There is nothing you can do that's wrong, okay?"

"Oh, I'm pretty sure there are things I can do that are wrong."

"Don't bite my dick off, but other than that, we're good."

I slid my hands to his waist. "No biting. Got it."

"I didn't say no biting, baby. Just don't bite my dick off."

"Ooh, kinky." I cocked my head. "Are we ready for kinky?"

"We're ready for whatever you're ready for, Trixie."

I bit my lip. "Don't bite dick off. Got it." I squared my

shoulders. "Okay, I'm ready."

He chuckled. "Remember, we can stop anytime you want to."

"I don't want to stop," I huffed out. "I just want to not feel guilty about sinning."

"You're not sinning."

"How do you figure?"

"Because I'm gonna make an honest woman outta you. Plus, look at it like we're doin' this biblically. We're fuckin' first, then we'll have the ceremony later. That's how they used to do it, right?"

I met his eyes and grinned. "Why, yes, yes they did."

"You gonna marry me?"

I raised an eyebrow. "Is this your proposal?"

"Yeah, baby, it is. We'll pick out the ring together whenever you want."

"Tomorrow?"

"Hell, yeah, we'll go tomorrow."

"Then, yes, I'll marry you."

His mouth landed on mine as he tugged the towel from my body and lifted me onto the bed. Dragging my hands above my head as he slid his tongue into my mouth, he cupped my breast with his free hand, rolling my nipple between his fingers.

I whimpered against his lips as he twisted my nipple one way, then the other, and I squeezed his hand holding mine, desperately wanting to move, but he wasn't budging. His mouth replaced his fingers and he finally let go of my hands before traveling down my body, kneeling between my legs, and spreading them before covering my very private part.

I writhed as he gently sucked on my clit and I fisted my hands in the duvet as he assaulted my nether regions. When his tongue slid inside of me, I couldn't help myself from bucking, which made him grip my thighs and keep me in place, but it did not make him remove his mouth. I let out a quiet frustrated groan as his tongue, then his finger, slipped inside of me and I was overwhelmed with the sensation. His mouth moved back to my clit and he slipped another finger inside of me and I cried out as I came.

He made a slurping noise and licked his lips with a grin. "Fuckin' vanilla, baby."

I blushed, dropping my head back with an embarrassed giggle.

He slid off the mattress and removed his jeans, rolling a condom on and hovering over me, completely naked.

"Oh my word, you're a giant," I squeaked. "I wasn't expecting you to be so big."

Spike grinned. "You know how to make a man feel good, baby."

I swallowed convulsively. "But how are you going to fit without tearing me in two?"

"I'm gonna get you ready again and we're gonna go slow." He settled his elbows on the bed beside my waist. "And if you need to stop, you tell me."

"Doesn't seem fair to stop before you get off."

He dropped his head to the comforter and his shoulders shook. I realized quickly that he was laughing and let out a scoff of derision. "*Why* are you laughing?"

He raised his head and met my eyes. "Because you just said 'get off,' and it was fuckin' adorable."

I frowned. "Are you teasing me?"

"No, baby, I'm not teasing you. Not maliciously." He ran a thumb over my bottom lip. "I think you're the sweetest thing on the planet, and the fact you're worrying about me when tonight is all about you, proves just how sweet you are." Leaning down, he kissed me gently. "I'm gonna make this good for you, sweetheart."

I cupped his face. "I trust you."

Sliding his hand between my legs, he slipped a finger inside of me as his thumb pressed against my clit and I arched against him, trying to get closer.

"Soaked, baby," Spike whispered, pulling his hand away, ignoring my irritated groan.

His cock pressed against my entrance, slowly pushing inside, stretching me, but not hurting me, and I gripped Spike's arms. His body was locked with the effort of going slowly, and he inched forward again, far enough he was now at my barrier.

"This is gonna hurt, Trix."

I nodded, squeezing my eyes shut. "Just do—"

He rocked forward and I whimpered as my virginity was torn from my body. Spike kissed me, stilling in order to give my body the time to get used to his invasion.

After a few seconds, he rolled us onto our sides, facing each other, and stroked my cheek. "We're gonna stay like this so you have the power. You move when you feel comfortable, okay?"

I nodded, sliding my leg up his outer thigh and over his hip. This brought me closer to his body and opened me up to him, which eased my discomfort and made me want more at the same time. "Are you okay?" I asked.

"Yeah," he bit out.

"Can you just take over, please?"

"I don't want to hurt you, honey."

"I'm okay, Spike. I just want this over."

"Romantic."

"That's not what I mean—oh!" I breathed out when he buried himself deep.

He slid his hand between us again, fingering my clit before starting to move. He rocked slowly at first, then faster and faster, harder and harder, all the while, continuing to work my clit with his fingers.

Rolling me onto my back, he was able to bury himself

deeper and harder, and I could feel an orgasm building. There was no pain, no discomfort, just ecstasy, and I wrapped my legs over his hips, lifting my body to match his motion, until I could no longer hold back my climax.

"I can't wait, honey."

"Go, baby," he ordered, and my walls contracted around him just as his cock pulsed inside of me.

He rolled us back onto our sides, pulling gently out of me and heading into my bathroom. "Don't move, Trixie," he called out.

Like I could if I tried.

I heard water running and then he returned with a warm washcloth, placing it gently between my legs. It helped ease the sting and I sighed with relief. Spike stretched out beside me. "When you feel up to it, you need to pee. It'll help you not get a UTI."

"A UTI?" I asked.

He pulled me over his chest. "Urinary tract infection."

"I know what a UTI is, honey, but why do I need to pee?"

"Because you are at a higher risk of getting one after sex."

I sat up slightly. "That's a thing?"

"Apparently." He slid his hand to my bottom and gave it a gentle squeeze. "I'll draw you a warm bath which'll help with the soreness."

"But I'm not sore."

"You might be," he countered. "I'm not taking any chances, so you're going to take a bath, drink some wine, and you're gonna rest. We can maybe watch a movie if you want, then we'll go from there."

"Are you always this bossy? Did I miss how bossy you were, or did I block it out because I've been in a fugue state, enamored by your eyes?" I sassed. "I'm fine. My vagina is perfectly fine, and since I'm the person attached to said vagina, I'm pretty sure I can take care of it without any advice from Dr. Spike, junior gynecologist."

He dropped his head back and laughed. "Okay, baby, I hear ya."

"Thank you."

He kissed me gently. "Now, how hot do you want your bath and do you want red or white wine?"

I rolled onto my back with a groan. "Jesse?"

"Right here, baby."

"Oh, never mind."

"Good choice." He sat up and slid off the bed. "Which wine?"

"Red, please. And popcorn. I want popcorn, extra butter, extra salt."

He chuckled. "Your wish is my command."

He headed into the bathroom and I heard the water start as I stayed on the bed, still unable to move. I'd lied before. I *was* sore, but it wasn't my nether regions that were hurting, it was the rest of my body. Sex was a workout and I hadn't worked out in years. I should probably start doing that or I was going to break a hip before I turned twenty-three.

SIXTEEN

BURNING SAINTS

Spike

I WAS IN Minus's office along with my Road Captain,
Sweet Pea, the club's VP, Clutch, and Ropes. I paced
the floor as I filled them in on Gary's situation.

"First of all, sit down before you wear a goddamned
hole in my rug," Minus said.

"Sorry," I said, taking a seat on the couch next to
Ropes.

"How much is Gary in for?" Minus asked.

I leaned forward, settling my elbows on my knees.
"Half a mil."

"Jesus Christ," Sweet Pea hissed.

"That's who he stole it from," I replied.

Clutch chuckled.

"There's no way in hell Edison is gonna let that slide," Minus said.

I nodded. "That's what I told Gary."

"You put some guards on their house?" Clutch asked Pea.

"I set up a rotation as soon as Spike called me," Sweet Pea said.

"And I've moved Trixie into a new place," I added.

Minus dragged his hand down his beard. "The club's got about two hundred thousand in reserves, but with two building projects coming up, plus no guarantee that Trixie's old man is good for it, I don't think I can swing a loan."

"I can cover the debt," Ropes said.

I raised an eyebrow. "You don't have to do that."

"It's not a big deal, really," he replied. "I can have the cash for you by tomorrow."

Ropes was a New York Times bestselling author ten times over, not to mention the fact he'd inherited a mint when his father died. Of course, you wouldn't know it by looking at him. However, spend any amount of time with him and you'd be bound to pick up on a certain layer of sophistication and style not typically attributed to club members.

"Even if I get him off the hook with Edison, Gary's about to be an unemployed church pastor," I pointed out. "It's gonna take the rest of his life just to make a dent in that kind of loan."

"You're not trying to straighten this man out with Edison for *his* sake. You're doing in for your woman, right?"

I nodded.

"We protect our own," Ropes said. "No matter what."

"Sounds like it's settled then," Minus said, rising to his feet. "Ropes will secure the loan, and you'll deliver payment to Edison," he pointed at me. "I want Sweet Pea to go with you as backup, but you'll take point."

We grunted and nodded in agreement and filed out of Minus's office.

I grabbed Ropes in the hallway. "Hey, man. You don't know what this means to me."

"Yeah, I do. That's why I offered," Ropes said. "Do you remember what I told you the day we first met? Back in that shitty motel?"

I nodded. "You said for most of the Burning Saints, the club was more like family than their own blood relations."

"That's right. So, that makes you my family. And if Trixie is your old lady, she's my family too."

"I'm gonna find some way to pay you back. I swear," I said.

"In the meantime, we'll get Edison paid, and you can decide how to deal with pastor Gary."

Ropes held out his hand for a shake, but I pulled him in for a hug. "Thank you."

* * *

I entered Aubergine Antiques and was immediately greeted by a well-dressed, attractive, brunette woman who looked to be in her mid-thirties. Other than the two of us, the shop appeared to be devoid of people. I carried a black duffel bag which contained five-hundred-thousand dollars in cash.

"Good evening, welcome to Aubergine. My name is Miranda, how may I help you?"

"I'm here to see Edison," I replied.

"I'm, sorry, but there's no one here by that name. Perhaps you—"

"Oleg Volkov," I interrupted. "I know he's here and I need to speak with him, now."

"Do you have an appointment?" she asked, dropping the pleasantries.

I spotted a security camera pointed directly at me and set the duffel bag down. I then unzipped it to reveal the contents. "Here's my appointment."

Just then the phone on Miranda's reception desk rang, which she answered. "Yes, sir. I'll send him right in," she said before hanging up.

"Please follow me," she said, leading me to the back of the showroom and through a door marked 'PRIVATE.'

As soon as I was through the door, two huge bodyguards, grabbed me, spun me around and were frisking me against the wall.

"He's clean, Boss," one of the guards said, in a thick Eastern European accent, as the other handed him the duffel bag.

I shook the guard off of me and straightened my kutte.

"Who the fuck are you?" Edison asked.

"Spike. I ride with the Burning Saints."

"I didn't ask who you ride with. Besides I can read," he said pointing to the club patch on my kutte.

"Yeah? Then how come you asked me for my name. It's right fucking here." I pointed to my name patch.

"Normally, I'd have Kevin break your jaw for your lack of respect," he said, pointing to the guard closest to me, "but this sack full of money has me intrigued."

"Your name is *Kevin*?" I asked the towering man, who let out a low growl in return.

"Why are you here, Spike of the Burning Saints?"

"I'm here to pay off Gary Mitchell's debt," I replied.

"There's half a million in cash in that bag. Which more than settles his tab with you."

Edison bobbed his head up and down. "This is good. Very good. I'm surprised, to be honest. I thought the pastor might try something stupid like involving the police, but instead he sends me a tough guy motorcycle man."

His guards laughed in unison.

Edison waved Kevin over to him. "Take this to the back room, inspect the bag for bugs or a tracking device, and count the money." He then turned to me. "Don't worry, Kevin won't be counting by hand. We have a machine, like the ones they have in Las Vegas. It'll only take about ten minutes."

"I can wait, but I'll tell you right now, if you've got anything stupid in mind, like making me disappear and keeping that money, I'd advise you squash that shit. My club knows I'm here, and they don't give a fuck about your politician friends."

Edison smiled. "I knew your club founder, Cutter. He and I did business together many times. And if this was still his club, I might be a touch intimidated by your words, but it's not."

"Don't let the good press fool you, Eddie. Minus is no teddy bear, and neither am I."

"You still haven't told me how a holy man came to employ your services," Edison said.

"Let's say I'm a friend of the family."

Edison grinned. "A friend of the preacher's daughter is more like it. Isn't that right?"

"You have the money. Leave the Mitchell family alone."

"Of course, of course. Once Kevin is done counting, I'll consider his debt paid in full. Then we can discuss your debt to me."

"What the fuck are you talking about?"

"The business license fee you owe me."

"How close to Chernobyl were you born?" I asked.

Edison rose to his feet. "If the pastor had come to me directly with my money, we'd be done with this by now. But he involved you in this transaction, and I don't know you. Those who I don't know, I don't trust. And, those who I don't trust, I don't do business with. So, in order for you to be involved in this transaction you must obtain a temporary license to do business with me. Such a license will cost you twenty percent of Mitchell's debt. That would mean you owe me one hundred thousand dollars. Payment is due within forty-eight hours."

"Sounds reasonable," I said. "Here's my counteroffer. Go fuck yourself."

"I could do that, but then the preacher's lovely daughter might not stay lovely for very long."

I took a step forward, shadowed by the remaining guard, and looked Edison square in the face. "You touch her, you die."

"A fighter, huh? Good," Edison replied. "How about you sing for your supper?"

"What the fuck are you talking about?"

"I need a middleweight fighter for a match this coming Saturday, and you look to be about one hundred seventy pounds."

"Why the hell would I agree to that?"

"Because, if you win, your debt to me is cancelled, and I'll even let you keep the purse. But if you refuse to fight, I'll sic your opponent on Christine Mitchell instead of you, and he'll take care of her outside the ring. Away from the judges."

* * *

"No, no, no. You're still too close to the bag. From there, all your punching power is coming from your shoulder.

If you take a few steps back, you can step inside while throwing the punch, utilizing your leg strength as well as your shoulder. Watch me."

Clutch demonstrated the technique several times. The snap of his gloves against the heavy leather bag reverberating throughout the otherwise empty gym.

"You, see?" he asked, changing places with me. "Now you try."

I took my stance, careful to mind my footwork and my left-hand position as I danced around the outside of the bag.

"Good. That's more like it." Clutch nodded. "Now, step in and snap that straight right."

I did as my coach instructed, feeling the full force of the blow resonate through every bone in my hand.

"You feel the difference?"

"Absolutely," I said, doing my best Sylvester Stallone.

"Alright, Rocky. Gimmie twenty-five of those in a row, and I want to see you do a full reset before each punch."

I nodded, took a deep breath, and started the drill. I'd only been training full time with Clutch for two days but was already sore in places I didn't know I had. I knew training was only going to get harder and tried to mentally pace myself while pushing my body to its limits. Everything I'd known about fighting up until now I learned in prison, but inmates play by a different set of rules than boxers. Inside, you use whatever means necessary to win a fight, because to lose one could very well mean losing your life. The only rule I ever saw observed in a prison fight was no shoes. Other than that, headbutting, eye gouging, biting, knees, and elbows were all fair play.

"I still can't believe you fucked up a simple pay off," Clutch said, with a chuckle.

"The pay off part went fine," I said, in between punches. "It was the part that came after that went all pear-shaped."

"Why the fuck did you agree to the fight?"

"I want him out of Trixie's life."

Clutch cocked his head. "And you think Edison will keep his word?"

I shrugged. "I'd say it's fifty-fifty odds."

"Better than your chances in this fight," he retorted.

"Hurtful," I dead panned. "Besides, how can you know my odds when we don't even know anything about the guy I'm fighting, other than he's a middleweight?"

Clutch sighed. "Another dumb move on your part."

"I figure he'll be a Russian tough guy with lots of tattoos, and a textbook mean mug."

My muscles began to burn and spasm as I neared the end of the drill.

"How's your chin?" Clutch asked.

"I've never been knocked out, if that's what you're asking."

"Twenty-five," Clutch called out. "That's it for the day. Sit down and I'll get your gloves off."

I plopped down on the wooden stool, and placed my gloved hands on my knees, palm up. Taking my gloves off was the best part of every workout. It meant I was done with Clutch's torture session, but it also meant a hot shower with Trixie was in my very near future.

"You think I've got a shot in this fight?" I asked.

"Of surviving?"

"C'mon asshole. Can you at least pretend to be my coach?"

"Alright, no jokes. You've got talent. Your height and weight are ideal for this weight class. Your cardio is strong, and you can swat pretty hard. Do you have knock out power inside those gloves? I dunno. But you're a hard worker, you're mentally strong, and you've got a shit ton of heart."

"Does that mean you're betting on me?"

Clutch laughed. "Fuck no. They're probably gonna lure their fighter out of his cage with raw meat seconds before the fight starts. You're gonna want your old lady to take a long look at that symmetrical face of yours before this guy turns it into a Picasso."

My coach was only half joking, and I knew it. Normally, I wouldn't be the least bit nervous to fight. I never went looking for trouble, but also never backed down from it either. The main differences between this fight and every other fight I'd been in were massive.

First, I didn't know my opponent. Every street or jailhouse fight I'd been in, I knew the guy I was fighting on some sort of personal level.

Next was the fact I'd be fighting in front of a betting audience.

And last was the biggest difference. Time. Hours and hours of time to think about the fight. It was almost enough to drive me crazy, but I stayed focused, and determined to not only survive this fight. I was going to fucking win it.

SEVENTEEN

BURNING SAINTS

Spike

WE ARRIVED AT the address Edison gave me
just before ten o'clock. His thriving fight
venue was, in truth, an abandoned Crisp-O's
potato chip factory near The Grotto that hadn't been in
operation since two thousand four. Cars were stacked in
the venue's makeshift parking lot, which was the only remaining paved section of land on the overgrown property. Loud, thumping music emanated from the place,
which was lit up like the fourth of fucking July. The place
was in a remote location, but not so remote that you

wouldn't want to be careful not to draw too much attention to the operation. I figured, if Edison was being this brazen with his fight club, someone within the Portland PD was getting paid.

We made our way inside and were shocked to see a venue that was sold-out, and then some.

"Every car out there must've been packed with ten fuckin' people," Minus shouted over the music.

The boxing ring was located in the center of what I assumed was previously the main factory floor. There were a few chairs circling the ring, but other than that, it was bare. Only a DJ booth, and two bars, which were serving beer and vodka only. The DJ was pumping Eastern European techno music at levels so loud, I thought I might get a concussion before I even stepped into the ring.

"Nervous yet?" Ropes asked.

"Just get me to the dressing room so I can puke and warm up," I replied.

We snaked our way through the crowd until we found a corridor which led to my dressing room. Although it didn't have my name on it, I assumed it was mine, because the words 'Dead Meat' were printed on the name plate. Inside the room, our accommodations were equally as dreary and welcoming.

"Good," Clutch said, dropping his duffel bag on the dusty floor. "They want a fight. Let's give 'em one."

Minus and Ropes helped Clutch set up a prep area and he was about to start taping me up when Edison and his two bodyguards came into the room.

"Spike, I'm so glad you decided to show up," Edison said, cheerily.

"Didn't sound to me like I had much in the way of options," I replied.

"Sure, you did. In fact, I'd say ninety-nine out of a

hundred men in your position would have opted to pay the business license fee."

"I don't buy my way out of fights."

"I don't think we've had the pleasure," Minus said, stepping in.

"No, I don't believe we have. Although I did business with your predecessor a handful of times. Of course, that's before the Burning Saints became real life Saints," Edison said with a greasy smile that made me want to punch *him* in the face.

"Don't let the good press fool ya," Minus said.

"Your boy said the exact same thing to me." Edison crossed his arms. "Interesting. I suppose we'll see just how much bite your little doggie has in him tonight."

"We doin' a weigh in?" Clutch asked. "I'd like to see who we're gonna fight tonight before the opening bell."

"No need to check weight," Edison said. "Your fighter is the same size as the man who was originally scheduled to challenge the champion."

"And that man is?" Clutch asked.

"I believe you met him the other night," Edison said to me, before pointing to the man on his left. "Kevin Arlovski is your opponent in tonight's fight."

"The truck nuts he is," Clutch growled.

"What's the problem?" Edison asked.

"He's a fuckin gorilla, that's the fucking problem," Clutch said.

"You told me this was a middleweight fight," I said.

"No. I told you I needed a middleweight fighter. After Kevin's original opponent dropped out, I was forced to find a suitable replacement. Lucky for you, you fit the bill."

"Lucky for me? You're out of your fucking mind. He's five inches taller and seventy-five pounds heavier."

"It's not my fault your mama only packed you one

lunch a day," Kevin said.

"See, the two of you are fighting already. How perfect," Edison said.

"The fight's off," Minus said.

"If Spike goes back on our agreement, his debt to me will double, and the time limit in which to pay me will be cut in half."

"He doesn't owe you shit," Minus said.

I scowled. "I can handle myself—"

"You stay quiet," Minus hissed, before turning back to Edison. "I should have never agreed to let him do this in the first place. This whole thing's bullshit."

"On the contrary, Mr. President. This is business. That crowd you hear out there isn't made up of boxing fans. It's made up of gamblers. People who have placed wagers of significant amounts in order to be here live on fight night. Not to mention the number of bets from those streaming the event from home or on their phones. I couldn't possibly leave all those people in the lurch."

"Sounds like a *you* problem," Minus said, clearly unshaken and unmoved by Edison's words.

"Fuck those degenerate assholes out there," I growled. "I'm here to keep you the hell away from Trixie."

"We don't need a boxing match to squash that," Minus said, clenching his fists. "In fact, why don't we just settle this shit right now."

"I told you this is my fight, not the club's," I said, standing in between Minus and Edison.

"Seems like your fighter should be left to make up his own mind. After all, he stands to make a great deal of money tonight, even though he will undoubtedly lose. I've promised Spike the challenger's purse of ten grand, and I don't welch."

"What about the winner's purse?" I asked.

"What Kevin will be paid is none of your concern."

"That's not what I asked," I said. "You sprung a heavyweight on me as my opponent, so you're gonna pay me double the champion's purse. I figure he's making at least three times what you're paying me."

"I make forty-five a fight," Kevin said.

"Thanks, big man," I said, turning back to Edison. "Ninety thousand dollars in my hand if I win."

Edison sighed. "You don't seem to understand. I didn't bring you here to fight, I brought you here to lose."

"You clearly don't know shit about me if you think I'd *ever* take a dive."

"Who said anything about taking a dive? I expect you to lose fair and square."

"Ninety thousand," I repeated.

Edison shrugged. "Sure, why not. There's zero harm in promising you something I'll never have to deliver."

"And you forget about the Mitchell family forever."

"You fight, I forget."

"Deal," I said, and we shook on it.

"What's this?" Edison asked, pointing to the tape on my wrist.

"I'm taping him up before I put his gloves on."

Edison laughed. "We only feature bare knuckle boxers at my events."

"Wait a damned minute," Clutch protested.

"Surely, that will not be a problem for your fighter?"

"No," I said as calmly as possible, while staring at Kevin's calloused meat hooks even as my mouth dried up like the Mojave Desert. "No problem at all."

"Good. We'll see you in the ring," Edison said before exiting with my opponent.

"Christ, kid. You sure you wanna do this?" Minus asked.

"What?" I asked, looking around the room. "None of

you have ever squared off with a guy who was bigger than you?"

"This is different," Minus replied.

"Damn right it is!" I shouted. "Street fights and bar brawls are pointless. This fight means something. I'm fighting for a purpose tonight."

Clutch put his hand on my shoulder. "That's what makes it so dangerous, kid."

"I will never back down from a fight."

Clutch nodded. "Alright. Let's get you warmed up."

* * *

Fifteen minutes later I was making my way through the crowd, towards the ring. My heart thumping loudly inside my chest as I danced and bobbed through the sea of faces. Once ringside, Clutch opened the ropes enough for me to enter the ring, as Ropes and Minus set up a stool and bucket by my corner.

"Remember your training," Ropes instructed. "Now isn't the time to get any crazy ideas. Just because this guy's bigger than we expected, we still stick to the game plan. Right?"

I nodded.

"What are the five Fs of fighting?"

"Footwork, fundamentals, fortification, and hit him in the fucking face."

"Fortification is the most important. Keep that left hand up at all fucking times. Stay covered. You hear me?"

"Got it."

"One more thing," Ropes said. "I just realized this is a real life Rocky versus the big ass Russian moment."

I grinned. "Rocky won that fight, didn't he?"

"Go get 'em, Stallion."

The crowd erupted into cheers as my opponent entered the room. The lights were brighter, and the music pumped up in volume for their local hero. The closer he got to the stage, the larger he became. While acting as Edison's bodyguard, Kevin's demeanor was calm, bordering on pleasant. Even back in the dressing room, he was almost docile. The Kevin moving towards me now, was practically foaming at the mouth. His pitch-black predator eyes, trained directly on me as he made his way into the ring.

Next to climb in were Edison and the referee, who motioned the fighters and trainers to move to the center of the ring. The music faded and the lights dimmed as Edison produced a wireless microphone from his inside jacket pocket.

"Ladies, Gentlemen, and everyone in between. Welcome to EBKB Super Fight Night Live!" he announced to thunderous applause and cheers.

"Nice to know he's an inclusive bloodthirsty gangster," I said to Clutch.

"Tonight," Edison continued, "We have a new challenger making his EBKB debut in the ring. Weighing in at a ready one hundred and seventy pounds, with a professional record of zero wins, zero losses. Fighting out of Portland Oregon, and representing the Burning Saints Motorcycle Club, in the blue corner, tonight's challenger in this main event title fight, Spike!"

The lack of fanfare made one particular spectator stand out to me. Sitting in the front row was someone wearing dark sunglasses and a John Deere trucker's hat, but even that disguise failed to hide Trixie from my eyes.

"What the hell is she doing here?" I asked Clutch, casually motioning to Trixie.

"Shit," Clutch said. "I sure as hell didn't invite her."

"Goddammit," I hissed.

"You've got to forget she's here. Block her out of your mind. Do you hear me?"

I nodded, but my eyes were still glued to her.

Clutch slapped me across the face. "Focus."

"I'm here," I replied, doing my best to forget Trixie had ringside seats to my murder.

"And in the red corner. Weighing in at two hundred and sixty-five pounds. With a professional record of seventeen wins, all by way of knockout or TKO. Your champion, Kevin 'The Mangler' Arlovski!"

"I'm sure the Mangler was just something his mother called him as a child. Nothing to worry about," Clutch said, handing me my mouth guard.

We stepped to the center of the ring where we were addressed by the referee.

"Alright, gentlemen. You both know the rules. No shots below the belt, no eye poking or gouging, no elbows, no intentional clashes of the head. You break when I say break, and you fight when I say fight. Obey my commands at all times and come out fighting when the bell rings. Now, hook 'em up and go back to your corners until the opening bell."

Kevin and I touched knuckles. The first, but not the last time the Mangler's fists would make contact with me.

We went back to my corner and Clutch gave me one last pre-fight "pep talk."

"The fight consists of three, three-minute rounds. If you're both still standing at the end, the decision goes to the judges."

"Who are the judges?"

"I'm not sure it matters. I don't think anyone's ever lasted all three rounds with this guy."

"You know you suck at this, right?"

"Stay covered up and don't die," he said, removing the stool and himself from the ring.

Ding! Ding! The opening bell rang out, and before I knew it, I was charging towards the center of the ring.

* * *

Trixie

Oh, crap. Did he see me?

I squeezed my eyes shut for a second and took a deep breath.

Calm down, your disguise is solid. He has no idea you're here.

I focused back on Spike and he looked my way.

He's looking right at me. Crap! He's definitely looking right at me. I'm so busted.

All of a sudden, Clutch slapped him across the face. Hard.

Why did Clutch hit him?

I was already melting down and the fight hadn't even started yet. I felt like I was gonna be sick. Why did Spike agree to do this and why didn't he tell me about it? I crossed my arms and huffed. Once I was done being worried sick about him, I was gonna be so angry.

Spike's opponent entered the ring, and my worry turned to pure fear. I'd never been to a boxing match or even seen one on TV. I'd seen clips of the all-time greats like Muhammed Ali, but that was about it. Given my limited knowledge and exposure to the sport, even I knew that both fighters were always roughly the same size. That was not the case in this fight.

The man introduced as the Mangler was considerably larger than the man I loved, currently standing opposite him. I'm sure the announcer said his full name, but all I caught was the Mangler part. My Spike was about to be *mangled*.

"You, okay lady?" the man next to me asked. His

breath stunk of beer and bad choices.

"Why wouldn't I be?" I asked, trying, and failing, to sound calm.

"For starters, you're dressed like you're at an Eric Church concert. And B, you've been wringing the shit out of your T-shirt since you got to your seat."

I looked down to see I'd practically destroyed the bottom of my shirt. I was sweating from every pore, and I was definitely going to be sick. But, before I could make a dash to the bathroom, the opening bell rang, and I was too petrified to move... or puke.

"Fight," the referee called out and Spike rushed at the giant.

"No, no!" I yelled. "Run away!" but, my voice was drowned out by the roar of the blood-thirsty crowd. Spike was like a Christian in Rome, thrown to the Lions to be torn apart for the sheer amusement of its citizens.

Spike threw the first punch. Or more accurately, punches. He went all 'Rock 'Em Sock 'Em Robots' on the Mangler as soon as he reached him, throwing punch after punch to his barrel-chested mid-section, but the larger man seemed unaffected by the barrage, keeping his hands high and doing very little to stop Spike's punches.

"Keep working the body! Let him show off! He'll get tired!" Clutch yelled from the corner.

I looked up at the fight clock, hoping the round was almost over, disheartened to see two minutes still remained in the round. It was at this time the Mangler seemed to grow tired of being Spike's punching bag and decided to fight back.

EIGHTEEN

BURNING SAINTS

Spike

I CHOPPED AWAY at Arlovski's mid-section for a good part of round one until he started swatting back. And I mean actual swatting. Like a bear, with his hands cupped like giant paws, he toyed with me while testing my range.

I did my best to stay on the inside, conserving my energy, throwing medium strength, but solid shots.

"I hope for your sake, you can hit harder than that," he taunted, as we circled each other.

"And I hope for your sake, they don't cancel 'the Reading Choo-Choo.'"

"You won't be able to read, write, or chew solid food when I'm through with you."

I made note of the fact that he wasn't wearing a mouth guard. I didn't hear a rule against it, and the ref didn't say anything when I popped mine in, so either my opponent has an iron jaw, or he's not expecting me to connect with it.

"Shut the fuck up and fight," the ref instructed.

Arlovski came at me with his first real punch of the fight. A looping overhand right, which I saw coming and successfully blocked. Even still, the force of the punch drove my left hand into the side of my head. It was a hell of a lot better than a direct hit, but still somewhat effective. I tried to return the favor with an uppercut, but this time it was him who blocked my shot.

I spent the rest of the round covering up and fighting at short range. I had to stay away from his power shots, which meant working from far outside or smothering him on the inside. My hands were already starting to go numb, which I suppose beats the alternative. But the pain of broken knuckles and swollen joints wouldn't come until after the fight. Right now, I had adrenaline and endorphins on my side, and they were about to go into overdrive.

* * *

Trixie

I don't think I took a single breath for the last minute of the round. The match looked like David and Goliath minus the sling, the stone, or any discernable help from God.

"Get out of there!" I yelled as the Mangler continued to bat Spike around the ring.

"You didn't bet on the new kid, did you?" the guy standing next to me asked.

"What if I did?"

"Then I'd say get used to the idea of not having that money anymore. Arlovski's undefeated."

"The new kid is my boyfriend," I said defiantly.

"Oh, shit. Then I'd say get used to the idea of not having a boyfriend anymore."

I huffed and gave him a dirty look. It was the best I could muster under the circumstances. Mercifully, the bell rang, and Spike had survived the first round.

I plopped down in my seat, elbows in my thighs, and rested my face in my palms. I didn't know how I was going to find the strength to watch two more rounds of this, or worse, see Spike knocked into a coma. So, I did what I always do when I'm scared and unsure of the future. I prayed. Not out of ritual or habit, or even because I thought my prayers swayed God's decisions about what happened here on Earth. I prayed because it helped put my problems into perspective. It humbled and centered me.

When I prayed, I thought about the struggle I was going through at that moment and tried to look at it from God's perspective. Through a birds-eye-view of the world as it was now, as well as the past and future. I thought of my pain and how insignificant it was in the grand scheme of the universe and I felt a little bit lighter. No problems solved, per se, but often having gained a greater perspective of them.

All of that being said, my prayers at that moment were simply for God to protect Spike from brain damage or death, and me from having a heart attack.

* * *

Spike

"Okay, kid. You made it through round one," Clutch said,

as he squeezed a sponge full of ice-cold water on my head. "How ya feeling?"

"Sorta like I'm getting beat up by a refrigerator," I replied.

"In this round, let's try to get hit a little less, whatta ya say?"

I rolled my eyes. Bad move, since it hurt like a mother fucker. "Ace game plan per usual, Coach."

"This guy thinks you're gonna work the inside all night. He thinks you've already given him the best you got. But you and me both know that isn't true. You got more gas in the tank than that tub of Russian gravy, and you haven't even begun to work from the outside."

"Ya, that wasn't strategic, I just don't wanna be anywhere near that guy's striking range."

"You're gonna have to be if you're gonna make enough space to put your hips and legs into your punches. That's the only way you're gonna hurt this guy. But you've gotta be smart and pick your moments."

I nodded. "You're right about his cardio. He was already breathing pretty heavily by the end of the round."

"That means he's gonna be looking for a knockout early in this round, so stay sharp. Get to the center of the ring and be the first one to get off a shot."

The bell rang, and this time Arlovski had a bit more pep in his step than at the start of the fight. He beat me off the line and delivered a sharp straight right hand just as I made it to the center of the ring. My nose stung and my eyes filled with water, making it nearly impossible for me to see. I didn't even see the next shot to my head coming, and it sent me straight to the canvas.

"Three...four...five..." I heard the referee counting. Scrambling to my feet as he continued. "Seven...eight."

"I'm up," I grunted. "I'm up goddammit."

The referee grabbed me by the wrists, checking my

strength and balance. "Are you okay to continue the fight?"

"Is *he*?" I asked, motioning to my opponent.

Kevin smiled and waved me toward him.

"Alright, fight," he called, and fight we did.

Arlovski threw another straight right, which I easily slipped. I controlled my breathing and focused on staying light on my feet. Another right hand thrown and slipped, followed by two missed jabs. This guy may have been bigger, but I was faster. I was still too close to throw a power punch but did my best to connect any time I could, while continually avoiding his shots.

The crowd began to grumble, then boo at their champion.

"Knock his ass out, Mangler!" a patron yelled out.

"What the fuck are you waiting for?" cried another.

The hecklers pulled Arlovski's focus for just a second, but that was all I needed. The moment his head turned towards the crowd I took a step backwards. By the time he turned back to me, I was already stepping forward with a right hand aimed at his jaw.

I connected, sending Arlovski backwards to the ropes, blood gushing from his mouth, his bottom teeth having cut through his cheek. I looked down at my hand to see teeth marks in my knuckles.

Some of the crowd's boos for Arlovski began to change into cheers for me, enraging my opponent.

"That's the last free shot you get," he said, wiping blood from his mouth as he moved toward me.

I covered up the best I could, but he got in some brutal body shots, that were definitely gonna see me pissing blood the next morning.

"Get the fuck outta there!" I heard Clutch yell, and it was only then I realized Arlovski had me trapped in a corner.

I turtled up the best I could, but he hit me with a hard body shot that almost sent me to the canvas for a second time.

"No!" I heard Trixie cry out above the roar of the crowd.

* * *

Trixie

Clutch and Ropes yelled frantically for Spike to get out of the corner, but the giant man inside the ring had other ideas. The Mangler rained down punches on a trapped Spike, who looked like he was struggling to stay covered up.

"Work out of the corner!" Clutch yelled just as the Mangler punched Spike in the gut. Spike doubled over, and for a split second, it looked like he might go down.

"No!" I screamed, pulling my sunglasses off, and throwing them to the ground.

I'd never been more terrified in my life.

Why was Spike doing this? Did he need money? Was it some sort of macho glory BS? None of this made any sense, and the worst part was, I may not ever get the chance to straighten it out with Spike because he'd likely be in a coma soon.

Spike locked eyes with me. It was brief, but it was clear he now saw me.

* * *

Spike

Every last bit of air left my body, and I lost the ability to take the next breath. My legs wobbled and my right hand was inches away from touching the canvas, earning my opponent a second knock down.

I glanced over to where Trixie was seated and caught her bright blue eyes. Beacons of pure light, surrounded by utter darkness.

Fuck this. I'm not gonna let myself get beat to death in front of the woman I love. I'm not gonna let another bunch of bully assholes tell me what I can and can't do with my fucking life!

Arlovski took a step back to let me fall. But this time I didn't go down. I re-planted my feet, blocked out the fact that I felt like I was drowning, and focused on my right hand. I imagined I was holding that old, rusty, railroad spike again. I recalled how it felt in my hand the day my fate had changed. I imagined it was even heavier now. That instead of being made of steel, it was made of my love for Trixie. Forged from something far tougher than molten iron.

Time felt like it had slowed down, but in reality, this all happened within seconds. Before I knew it, I'd stepped forward, and delivered an uppercut with everything I had. My new spike in hand. Fighting for her. Fighting for us.

* * *

Trixie

I was in shock. In complete disbelief at what I had just seen with my own eyes.

Spike was seconds away from defeat when, from out of nowhere, he punched the Mangler so hard, the giant stiffened and fell backwards like a fallen oak tree. Spike looked battered and dazed as the referee began counting down from ten all the way down to one.

The crowd went crazy. Bottles, cans and just about everything else flew into the ring, as Spike was announced as tonight's winner and new champion. I took this as my cue to get out of the crowd before a riot broke out.

* * *
Spike

I was still catching my breath as Ropes and Clutch hustled me back to the dressing room.

"What the fuck h…happened back there?"

"You won kid, that's what happened," Ropes said.

"Trixie! She's here somewhere," I said. "Someone needs to find her and make sure she's okay."

"I'm on it," Minus said, before taking off back toward the ring.

"Holy shit," I said, trying to replay the last few minutes in my mind.

"More like deep shit," Clutch said as we reached the dressing room.

He opened the door to reveal Edison standing with his one remaining bodyguard.

"Like I said," Clutch grumbled.

"What the fuck was that?" Edison shouted.

"You heard the referee. That was our fighter beating your fighter," Clutch said.

"That wasn't the deal," Edison seethed. "Spike was supposed to lose."

"I told you not to bet against me," I said.

"Don't get cute with me, punk," Edison said.

"You made the match," Clutch said. "It was your fight. So don't get all pissy just because you lost."

Edison jammed a finger in my face. "You cost me a lot of money tonight, and I'm not gonna forget that."

"You'll forget about it or I'll fuckin' make you forget." Clutch took a step towards Edison and was met by his bodyguard. "Unless you're about to ask me to dance, I'd back the fuck up, big boy."

The bodyguard stayed in place, opening his jacket to

200

reveal a holstered pistol.

Clutch's face lit up. "Oh, shit. Is that a Colt 1911 with the white pearl grips?"

"Yeah," the guard grunted.

"Whoa, can I see that?" Clutch asked, taking a step forward, and cold cocking him in the jaw. The bodyguard flew backward toward Ropes who took him to the ground and disarmed him, tossing the gun to Clutch.

Clutch grabbed Edison and pressed the gun against his forehead. "Make a move and I give this place a badly needed paint job," he called out to the bodyguard.

"Do what he says," Edison instructed.

With the bodyguard now subdued, Clutch turned his attention back to Eddison. "You were warned not to fuck around with us, but you didn't listen, did you?"

Edison's jaw tightened.

"We agreed to a fair fight, for the winner's purse, and Spike knocked your guy's dick in the fucking dirt. Now, instead of asking us how we'd like payment, you're trying to stiff us."

"Spike owed me. This fight was his payment. We're even now."

"The hell we are," I said. "You owe me ninety grand."

"Plus twenty percent extra as a penalty for fucking with the Burning Saints. That's one hundred and eight thousand in cash, tonight."

"Fuck you," Edison replied. "This is my place, and we play by my rules."

"Okay. If that's the way you wanna play it. This is *his* gun," Clutch said, motioning to the guard, "Shooting you in *your* foot."

Clutch fired a round straight down. The .45 caliber bullet tearing a hole through Edison's right foot, sending him to the floor, screaming.

"Now, you're gonna give my fighter what you owe

him, or I'll do the other foot. Or maybe I'll blast a body part you care even more about," Clutch said, pointing the gun at Edison's crotch.

"I have the money," he panted between agonized groans.

"Where?" Clutch asked.

"There's a… s…safe is in my office. Down…t…town."

"On your feet, big boy," Clutch ordered the body-guard. "You're gonna carry your boss out to our van," he said, before turning his attention back to Edison. "And then you're gonna take Ropes to your office, where you will pay him in full. Once that's taken care of, he'll drop you off at the emergency room. Any further fucking around on your part will result in your immediate death. Plain and simple. Got it?"

Edison nodded.

Clutch turned to Ropes. "I'm gonna call in a couple guys to back you up. I'll have them meet you at the van."

"What about Minus?" Ropes asked. "He's not gonna be happy about this."

"Under fucking statement of the year," Clutch replied. "Just try to get pegleg here to the van without Minus seeing you and I'll take care of the kid."

NINETEEN

Trixie

I MADE A mad dash for my car, tears making it hard to see as I did. I slid into the driver's seat and started the engine, calling Gemma as I pulled out of the parking garage.

"Hey, lovey, how are you this fine evening?"

"Can you meet me?" I asked on a sob.

"Fucking hell, what did the wanker do?"

"Can you just meet me at home?"

"Of course, love. Give me twenty minutes."

We hung up and I continued to my condo, pulling into

the parking garage and hearing the sound of motorcycle pipes following me. I glanced behind me as the gate opened, ready to get out and fight a biker, but whoever he was drove away and I continued to my parking spot.

I made my way up to my home and headed inside, opening a bottle of wine just before my doorbell pealed. Gemma was early and the second I opened the door, I burst into tears again.

"What the hell happened?" she demanded, closing the door as she pulled me in for a hug.

It took me several minutes to calm down enough to be able to speak. Gemma held me until I could hiccup out, "He was *fighting!*"

"Fighting?" she asked. "Fighting with whom?"

I filled her in on everything I knew and it only seemed to confuse her more.

"Are you saying he was competing at an underground fight club?" she asked.

"Yes."

"How did you even find out about the fight?" Gemma asked.

"I went to the Sanctuary to surprise him, and Tacky was at the gate. He said he was surprised to see me, he thought I'd be at the fight already to cheer Spike on. I had no idea what he was talking about, but I played dumb and told him I misplaced the address and had hoped to catch him and follow him over. Luckily, Tacky isn't the sharpest knife in the drawer and was more than happy to tell me where the fight was."

"Bloody hell, love, you always know just enough to get you into trouble."

"This isn't my fault, Gemma. This is Spike's. He was getting beat to hell on purpose!"

"Did he say why?"

I shrugged. "Probably for money, Gemma."

"He's a welder, right?"

I nodded.

She frowned. "Doesn't he *make* quite a bit of money?"

"So?"

"*So...* why would he need to fight for money?"

"I don't know." I threw my hands in the air and stomped into the kitchen. "Maybe he was doing it for fun... which is worse."

"Sweetie, does Spike seem like the kind of person who would be at an underground fight club just for fun?"

Before I could answer, my doorbell pealed, and I scowled. "Who could that possibly be?"

"I'll get it," Gemma offered, and made her way to the door.

My building had security and the only way to get up was to be on a list, so the only people who could knock on my door without a courtesy call would be other residents, Gemma, my brothers, or Spike. Not even my parents had access.

"If it's Spike, don't open it."

Gemma glanced through the peephole before opening the door, then one by one, the Burning Saints' women filed through the door. First Cricket, followed by Gina, Devlin, and Callie.

"Looks like the cavalry has arrived," Gemma said, closing the door behind them.

"What on earth?" I whispered.

"Heard you had a little fright," Cricket said, removing her incredibly stylish leather jacket and setting it over the arm of my sofa before pulling me in for a hug.

"I think that's an understatement, Cricket," I argued. "Do you know what he was doing?"

"I do."

"Why would he *do* that?"

She wrapped an arm around my shoulders. "Why don't we go and chat while the ladies pour the wine?"

Cricket led me down the hall to my little office overlooking the water. There wasn't much furniture in there yet, but my favorite high-backed chair was there and Spike had found the matching one online that had arrived the day before yesterday, so he'd put it together for me. Eventually, the plan was to put floor to ceiling bookshelves and fill it with books and some of Spike's sculptures so that it could be a place for me to read.

Cricket moved one of the chairs so it was facing the other and smiled. "Have a seat, honey."

I lowered myself into my chair and linked my fingers together while she faced me. "What's going on?"

"Do you know why Spike was fighting tonight?"

I bit my lip. "Honestly? No."

"But your mind's running rampant with the possibilities, right?"

I grimaced. "Yes."

She gave me a gentle smile. "Well, sweetie, whatever you're coming up with, it's worse."

I gasped. "How could it possibly be worse?"

"Because he's fighting off the debt your father created."

Cricket filled me in on the *entire* story. Everything. The bad, the ugly, and the worse. I sat and I listened, the bile filling my throat threatening to spill with every word and not just because of what she was telling me.

But because of how I'd treated Spike. These people my father had 'gotten in' with had betrayed Spike at the last minute and he still did the fight in order to protect me and my stupid father.

My whole life, my parents touted that the 'way of the church' was the only way, and the world was dangerous and of the devil. Yet, here was this group of 'sinners' who had given of themselves, their safety, and their love to help them, and me, when they could have just left us to rot.

"Oh my word," I bit out, now sobbing uncontrollably, unable to breathe, almost to the point of hyperventilating.

"Honey, it's going to be okay," Cricket crooned.

"I don't understand why he just didn't tell me," I said once I calmed down a little.

"One of the things about being an old lady is that there will be times they can't, or won't, tell us everything. Sometimes they will tell us just enough to assuage or frustrate us, or they'll tell us everything. But, honey, there will be times we don't want to know. Trust me." She took one of my hands and squeezed. "This life can be difficult at times, I get it, but I promise, it's so worth it."

I nodded. "I get that part of it. I just don't understand, considering all of this was about me and my family, why he didn't tell me himself. I mean, *you* know, why wouldn't *I* know?"

"I know because Minus is the president, and I'm not only his wife, I run the club with him. The other ladies only know what their men have told them, and, honestly, I doubt they've said much. As a rule, we don't talk about a lot of club business amongst ourselves. Once you and Spike chat, and you feel like you want to talk, vent, whatever, you're welcome to share with the rest of them, but it's your story, so it's up to you. We are a vault, Trixie, and we will always have your back. I'm sharing because Minus asked me to come and told me I could tell you everything. He saw you run out of there so upset and couldn't reach you, and he had a feeling you'd need me. Spike doesn't know we're here, but I think he'll be glad we are."

"Well, I certainly am." I squeezed her hand. "Wait.

Minus saw me leave?"

Cricket nodded. "Yes. He sent Tacky to follow you home."

"Oh," I breathed out. "That makes more sense now."

"Trixie!" I heard Spike bellow. "Get out of my way, Gemma. Trixie!"

"Time for his come to Jesus meeting." Cricket smiled, rising to her feet. "I'll send him in, okay?"

I nodded, wiping my tears.

Spike rushed into the office a few seconds later, his face a lot less bloody than when I'd left him, but still very swollen and bruised, despite being bandaged.

"Baby." He knelt in front of me and dropped his cheek to my thighs. "Fuck, please don't leave me."

"What?"

"Don't leave me."

"Honey, I'm not going to leave you."

He raised his head. "You're not?"

"No way." I frowned. "Why would you think I'd leave you?"

"Because everyone leaves me." He sighed. "And you were so mad."

"Yes, I was angry because I was worried, and I obviously didn't have all the information. Cricket filled me in and now I'm even more in love with you, but a little more irritated with you, because you should have told me, but I also understand why you didn't tell me which irks me to no end."

"Huh?"

"You should never have gone to that fight. My father should have been the one in the ring with that Mangler guy. *He* should have been the one getting his brains beat out by him. Not you." I slid my hands into Spike's hair. "I can't believe you went to those lengths to protect him... and me. It's, well, beyond everything, honey."

"Haven't you figured out I would do anything for you?"

"I thought I had," I admitted. "Now I know it's even more."

"I love you."

"I love you, too." I went to squeeze his hand, and he hissed in pain. "Are you bruised?"

"Pretty sure they're broken."

"Oh my word, why are you not at the hospital?"

"Ah, because my woman rushed out in a snit, sobbing her eyes out, and that took priority."

"I was not in a snit," I hissed, pushing up from my seat. "I was upset because my *man* didn't have the decency to tell me everything. Something that I hope he will think twice about in the future. Come on, let's get you to the emergency room."

He stood and shook his head. "No."

"No? What do you mean, no?"

"Eldie will fix me up."

"Who the heck is Eldie?"

"Gina." He smiled. "Her nickname's L.D. for lady doctor. She's got a clinic close to the club. She takes care of all of us."

"I have so misjudged all of you, haven't I?"

"Have you?" he challenged.

"Well, no, not personally, but people outside of the church in general, I think."

"No you haven't."

"Why do you say that?"

"Baby, when I met you, you were in a room full of, for lack of a better term, teenage hoodlums, and you smiled and laughed, and welcomed us all without a fake anything about you. Then, when I ran into you on the street, you walked into that tattoo shop and spoke to everyone in there like they were your equal. Then, despite

209

the fact you've been raised to believe the gays are gonna bring the world down, you treat your brother and his partner like they are the most amazing people on earth."

"Because they are," I rasped.

"Yeah, but you could easily allow the teachings of the Bible or the church or whatever to cloud your judgment and you fight that, baby. You fight it every day." He slid his arms around my waist and kissed me gently. "I'm so fuckin' proud of you. I'm proud to know you, proud to have you on my arm, and unbelievably humbled that you would even think that I'm worthy of your love."

"Spike," I whispered, blinking back yet more tears. "I'm the one that's humbled. You're so much smarter than me and you love with your whole being. I've never known anyone whose love was as unconditional as yours. You teach me so much about myself and others every day and I can't wait to find out more as we grow old together." I stroked his cheek. "I'm so sorry I ever doubted you."

Suddenly what sounded like two grizzly bears fighting in the wild erupted from the next room.

"*What* is that?" I asked.

"I believe that would be the sound of Minus discussing how the Edison situation was handled by Clutch."

"We better get out there and make sure they don't break anything."

Kissing me, he gave me another squeeze before hissing out in pain again. "Fuck."

"Oh, honey," I breathed out. "We need to get you looked at."

He nodded, and we headed out of my office.

Walking out to my great room to find a bevy of bikers sitting on my sofa eating food and drinking beer that I did not have in my kitchen previously, it looked as though Minus and Clutch had worked out whatever they needed to work out, so I relaxed a little bit.

Gina headed our way immediately. "Clutch said you might have some broken bones in your hands."

Spike nodded, reaching his hands out so she could examine him. I shuddered with every grimace and painful hiss Spike let out, continuing to resist Gemma's attempt to pull me away from him as Gina poked and prodded him.

"Come and get some wine, love," Gemma insisted, but when Spike nodded his agreement, I finally let her lead me away.

About twenty minutes or so later, Gina and Spike joined me in the kitchen where she set a backpack on my island. "Spike's got a couple of broken knuckles on his right hand. The left is more bruised than anything, so I'm going to show you how to tape him up because there really isn't any other way for him to heal, other than to keep him immobilized, sound good?"

I nodded, feeling the blood drain from my face.

She smiled. "Don't worry, honey, it's really easy, and I'm always around if you need anything. I'm also going to prescribe him some painkillers."

"Okay, Gina, thanks."

Before she walked me through how to wrap his hands, Spike needed to stand at the island with ice packs covering his knuckles for a few minutes and he did so, laughing with his brothers, despite his pain.

I took this reprieve to take a look around me and be in the moment. Forget (just for a moment) that the love of my life was beat to crap because of something my father did, and feel the love surrounding us.

I was suddenly part of something. A family, if you will. One that I could never have expected would be so amazing. You have Minus and Cricket, the patriarch and matriarch of the family, who as soon as they knew there might be something wrong with me, came running to fix what was broken.

And then there was crazy Uncle Clutch and saintly Auntie Eldie, followed closely by the high-achieving 'cousins' Sweet Pea and Callie who were not only both attorneys, but looked like they should be on the cover of a fitness magazine.

And most of all, Ropes and Devlin who had become more than just close friends and employers, they were like another older brother and sister to me, and I know Spike felt the same.

Spike met my eyes and smiled.

"You okay?" he mouthed, and I nodded, closing the distance between us.

"Are *you* okay?" I asked, peeling off one of the ice-packs and leaning in to look at his knuckles. They were bright red and starting to purple. "Ooh, that looks painful, honey."

"The beer's helping."

"Time's up," Gina said, handing me the wrap. "You ready for me to show you how to do this?"

I nodded and we spent the next few minutes binding Spike's hands. I had to give him credit, he barely made a sound and it had to have hurt.

After a quick trip to the all-night pharmacy to pick up his pain meds with Gemma (who once again supported me in everything), we returned home to find everyone gone and my place cleaner than when they'd arrived.

"I'm going to get going," Gemma said.

"You can stay," I countered.

"You don't have to go on my account, sweetheart," Spike said.

"I just got the spare bedroom set up." I smiled. "Stay, sleep in. I'll make French toast in the morning."

"I don't do mornings, love, but if you're offering in the afternoon when I actually wake up, I'll stay."

I chuckled. "You got it."

"Okay, then. Thank you."

"I'll grab you pajamas."

"You know I sleep in the buff."

"Ah… not while Spike's here, you don't."

She wrinkled her nose. "Right. Sorry."

Spike laughed. "I'm gonna hit the hay. You two can figure shit out without me."

"Okay, honey, I'll meet you in there," I said, turning back to Gemma. "I'll bring something for you to your room."

"Sounds good. Thanks, love."

I grabbed her a pair of giant sweatpants and an even bigger T-shirt, because even though I loved my best friend, I wasn't blind and neither was my man, and she needed to be covered up as much as possible because she was *gorgeous*.

"All set?" Spike asked, once I walked back into my room.

"Yep."

He smirked.

"What?" I asked.

"You know it wouldn't matter."

"What wouldn't matter?"

He shrugged out of his T-shirt. "If Gemma walked around buck-naked."

"I don't want to tempt fate."

"Baby, you're not hearing me."

I huffed, moving to pull my side of the bed down.

"Trixie, look at me."

I met his eyes and he smiled. "She could strip down in front of me, and my dick would stay as soft as it is right now."

I pulled off my T-shirt with a huff.

"Okay, not so soft anymore."

I bit my lip and blushed, feeling more irritated with myself for feeling insecure than I did about being unclothed in front of Spike.

"Am I ever going to stop feeling *less than*?"

"I fuckin' hope so, honey," he said. "But you don't ever have to worry because I'll remind you every day if you forget."

I skirted the bed and made my way to him, dropping my head to his chest and wrapping my arms around his waist. "I love you."

"Love you too, baby. Gonna need your help getting me out of these jeans, though. My dick's hard and my hands are wrapped too tight to work the button."

I couldn't stop a quiet snort-laugh as I looked up at him. "Does that mean I can try and, um, give you a blow job?"

"Fuck." His nostrils flared as he took in a deep breath. "Yeah, baby, you can absolutely do that."

I clapped my hands and stepped back, finally noticing the bruises on his torso. I gasped. "Oh my word." I gently touched one of the bruises on his ribs and he leaned away from me. "How bad does this hurt?"

"Not bad," he said, but I was sure he was lying.

"I think we should wait."

"Oh, hell no. We're not waiting on my account. If you've changed your mind, that's one thing, but—"

"No, I've actually wanted to for a while."

He raised an eyebrow. "You have?"

I blushed. "Yes, but I don't want to hurt you, Spike."

"I just took a pain pill, baby. I'm feelin' no pain. And your lips wrapped around my dick is gonna be nothin' but a delight."

I settled my hands on his shoulders… about the only place that didn't have a bruise, and asked. "Are you sure?"

"I'm fuckin' sure."

I nodded and helped him remove his jeans and boxer briefs before kneeling in front of him.

I really had no idea what I was doing but Gemma had given me a rather quick rundown of the basics and had sent me a link to one of her favorite naughty movies. I'd watched about twenty seconds of it and slammed my laptop closed as I stood with my freezer door open in an attempt to cool my heated cheeks before returning to my laptop and forcing myself to do 'research.'

I looked up at him. "You'll tell me if I do something wrong, right?"

"Just don't bite my dick off and you'll be good."

I rolled my eyes. "Helpful, honey, thanks."

I wrapped my hand around his cock and stroked gently before covering the tip with my mouth. I took him deeper and Spike settled his hands on my head as I gripped his length gently and pulled down, taking him further.

He groaned as I continued to work his cock with my mouth and hand. I cupped his balls, taking him all the way to the back of my throat, moving my hand faster and faster as I almost gagged myself.

"Baby, I'm gonna come," he warned.

I pulled back. "What do I do?"

"Depends on if you want to spit or swallow," he rasped.

I licked my lips. "I'll try anything once."

I wrapped my lips back around him and he moved against my mouth, his body locking and his cock pulsing against my tongue as warm liquid slid down the back of my throat.

"Jesus H. Lucifer Christ," Spike bit out.

I stood unable to meet his eyes. "Was that okay?"

"Did you obey the first and only rule?"

"I did not bite your… ah… dick off."

He cupped my face and kissed me. "Did I come?"

"Um, yes."

"Did it take a long time for me to come?"

I smiled. "Um, I don't think so."

"Okay, so that's kind of an indication that I fuckin' loved it, baby."

I let out a sigh of relief. "I did good?"

"Baby, it was amazing."

"Okay, good, because I *loved* it."

"You did?"

I nodded. "And I really want to do it again. I've heard women say it's, like a chore and stuff, so I was a little worried, but it's so fun."

"Fuck, you really are the perfect woman."

"Well, if doing that on the regular makes me perfect, sign me up."

He laughed, kissing me again, before heading into the bathroom to clean up. We went about our nightly routine to get ready for bed before climbing under the covers and snuggling close.

Well, as close as we could without me injuring him further.

TWENTY

BURNING SAINTS

Trixie

ALMOST FOUR MONTHS later, I had a surprise
planned for Spike, and I was starting to melt
down with the stress of it all.

Albeit, internally.

I was sitting at the reception desk at work, and a hand
landed on my shoulder, making me jump a mile.

"Shit, sorry, honey," Devlin said.

"No, it's okay. It's me," I rushed to assure her. "I'm
just…"

"Worked up because of tonight?"

I sighed. "Yes. Exactly."

"He's going to love it!"

"Do you think so?"

She leaned against the desk and settled her hands on her belly. "Why wouldn't he?"

"Oh, I don't know, maybe because I didn't tell him I was having the boys go and raid his place and steal his stuff without his permission?" I bit my lip and looked up at her. "Maybe he won't like it."

She reached over and squeezed my arm. "Trust me, honey. He's gonna love it."

"I hope so," I breathed out.

The bell over the door rang, indicating Devlin's client was walking in, so she took him back and I focused on the last few things I needed to finish up before I could leave.

Jenson walked his client through the velvet drapes about twenty minutes later and leaned over the desk once she'd left. "Hey, sissy."

"Hi. Your client looked happy."

"She did."

"She also looked like she wanted to jump your bones."

He laughed. "She made that very clear."

I wrinkled my nose. "How often does that happen?"

"You don't want to know." He tapped his fingers on the top of the desk. "I want to run something by you."

I stopped what I was doing and focused on him. "Everything okay?"

"Yeah. Ah, I was thinking about prospecting with the Saints."

I opened my mouth in shock, then closed it again because I wasn't sure what to say.

"Shit, it's a bad idea," he rasped.

"No." I cleared my throat, standing and making my

way around the reception desk. "No, it's amazing!" I squealed, wrapping my arms around him.

"Really?"

"Yes." I leaned back and met his eyes. "But what brought all of this on? Is it sudden? It seems sudden."

"It's not sudden." He smiled, releasing me. "I watch how Spike is with you, and I watch how Ropes is with Devlin, and the way they helped Dad. Jesus, Chris, they bailed that asshole out."

"I know," I whispered.

"He didn't deserve that."

I bit my lip. "I'm beginning to agree."

Minus signed off on Ropes' agreement to pay the church back for every penny my dad stole. In exchange, my father agreed to use his political influence at the club's behest. His indiscretion would be kept out of the public eye, provided he never worked for, or built, another church ever again. It was made very clear that if my father should so much as start a men's Bible study, the agreement would be made null and void, and he'd be hung out to dry.

Of course, Jenson wasn't privy to that information, and I couldn't tell him, so until he was a fully patched member of the club, I had to keep the first secret I'd ever kept from my brother.

"And then they made sure Celeste had a place after Mom and Dad decided they couldn't afford the mortgage," he said.

I nodded. My parents had decided to rent their palatial house out and move to a smaller home in Baker City. I mean, this all took weeks. Without any consideration for us, they just pulled up stakes and left. They could have moved over the bridge to Vancouver and found something smaller there, closer to Mattias and Ronnie, staying closer to me and Jenson, but, no. They moved over four hours away, touting the inability to find anything appropriate close by. Don't get me wrong, Baker City was gorgeous, especially in the winter when it snowed, but my parents were not a reason to visit.

After Celeste had been dismissed, Minus and Cricket set her up at their home. They had a sprawling farmhouse on four acres (which had been expanded by another six when they bought the adjacent property two years ago). They'd been in the process of building four tiny homes and turning a rundown barn into a bunkhouse for troubled youths, but one of the tiny homes was done and they gave it to Celeste, promising she'd have it until she either died, or chose to leave. Even if she didn't work for them anymore, she was welcome to stay.

To say these people were generous beyond belief was an understatement.

"I know, that was crazy, right?" I whispered.

Jenson nodded.

"I think if you want to be part of the club officially, it'll be amazing." I smiled. "Who are you going to ask to vouch for you?"

"I was thinking about talking to Spike. Do you think he'd do it?"

"If he doesn't, I will murder him." I chuckled. "But you know he will."

Spike and Jenson had become like brothers and it was the most amazing thing watching the two of them together. We tried to do some kind of family dinner once a week with Mattias and Ronnie, either at their place or ours, then Jenson and Spike had a standing beer night while I went out with Gemma.

Then, of course, there was usually some kind of a girls' night with the club women, which we all called, 'bible study' since Wednesday nights were 'church' for the men. We'd gone so far as to start referring to ourselves as the 'church ladies,' much to the chagrin of our men. It amused us immensely, so it wasn't changing anytime soon.

Jenson grinned. "I'll talk to him tonight."

"Perfect," I said.

"I'll let you finish your shit. Am I walking you down?" he asked.

I shook my head. "I think Spike's picking me up and we're eating before."

"Okay, sissy, I'll see you there."

I nodded, and he headed back behind the curtains.

Luckily, I was busy enough that my mind was occupied, which meant the rest of the day flew by quickly.

* * *

"Baby, where are we goin'?" Spike asked as I led him away from my car.

"This way."

"I thought you wanted to go home and take a hot bath." He squeezed my hand as we walked.

"Oh, I do, but we just need to make a quick stop first." I smiled up at him. "Is that okay?"

"Of course, baby. Do what ya gotta do."

We continued down the sidewalk, ending at Room 191 Gallery.

"An art gallery?" Spike asked, pulling the door open for me.

"Yes, Gemma's friend owns it."

"You buyin' some art?"

"Something like that," I said, evasively.

He cocked his head and followed me in, then stalled as his gaze swept the space. His sculptures were meticulously staged around the room and they looked incredible.

"Jesus," he breathed out. "What's going on, Trixie?"

"Oh my gosh, please don't be mad," I begged.

"What is this? I need you to start talking, honey."

"Gemma's friend owns this place, like I said, and I asked Gemma to talk to him about maybe giving you a showing. I took some photos of your stuff and sent it to him and he went gaga over it, wanting all of it, so I made a plan with the guys to move it without you knowing and here we are." The words flew out of my mouth like an auctioneer, ending with a triumphant, "Tada."

"You brought all of my sculptures here?"

"Not the one you did for me. That one is mine, so, no, not all of them." I squeezed my eyes shut before opening just one. "Are you mad?"

He studied me for a few seconds before looking around again, then pulling me close. "I'm not mad."

"Are you sure?"

"Yeah. I'm happy. I'm not gonna lie, I'm scared shit-less, and I'm fuckin' overwhelmed."

I slid my arms around his waist and squeezed. "In a good way?"

"Yeah, baby, in a really good way."

"Spike!"

We turned to see Ropes and Devlin rushing toward us, followed by the rest of the guys and their women, and two people I recognized but had never met in person.

"Fuck, Doozer?" Spike said with a laugh.

The big man pulled him in for a hug. "I wasn't about to miss this."

"Hey, Trouble," Spike said, pulling the petite woman in for a hug. "This is Trixie."

"Oh my god, hi," she said, hugging me. "I've heard so much about you."

"You have?"

"Are you kidding me? Spike has been pining for you

for*ever*."

I blushed, leaning against Spike as he wrapped an arm around my waist. "Okay, let's not spill *all* my secrets."

"I'm not sure that was much of a secret, honey," I pointed out.

He kissed the top of my head. "Maybe not."

"Your stuff is really good, Spike," Trouble said. "I can't believe I didn't know you sculpted."

"Thanks, sweetheart. It's something I've always done as a stress relief." He gave me a squeeze. "Hadn't thought about displaying it."

"Spike, love," Gemma walked up behind us, and we turned to find her with Philippe, the gallery curator. "This is Philippe Holte, he's the man behind the gallery."

"Mr. Holte, I don't know what to say. Thank you for all *this*," Spike said.

"Please call me Philippe, and let me assure you, the pleasure is all mine. Your work is breathtaking. It's unlike anything I've seen."

It was finally time for Spike to blush. His ears reddened, followed by his neck and cheeks, as Philippe piled on the praise.

"Since this was a surprise, I took the liberty of valuing each piece myself. I hope you don't mind. Don't worry about the prices listed on each piece. Those are merely opening bid numbers, and I can make any changes you'd like."

Spike looked at the price listed on the sculpture next to him and choked, "Um, Philippe. I think you've got an extra zero on this one."

Phillipe let out a controlled laugh. "True modesty in an artist is a rare thing. Take my advice. Whatever you do, hide those kinds of feelings way down deep inside. They will not serve you well in the art industry."

Spike smirked and nodded as he squeezed my hand.

"Your work is superb as is, but the buyers are going to lose their minds over you. I'm expecting big numbers from this auction, and it behooves the gallery to make it so."

"What's the house's cut?" Spike asked.

"Twenty percent to the gallery and five to me, with an additional two percent should every piece sell for at least the opening bid amount."

"Fair enough, but I wouldn't go picking out your yacht just yet. I'm just a welder. I'm not really an artist."

"You can't be for real," Philippe said, turning to me. "Is this guy for real?"

I smiled and nodded. "He's exactly what you see."

"Well, I guess we'll find out tonight, won't we?"

"Tonight?" Spike asked, his rosy cheeks turning white.

We turned to see a small group of well-dressed people walk through the gallery doors, and as I suspected, they walked straight to the sculpture by the window. It was about six-feet tall and was in the shape of a horse made with giant gears and washers. It was magnificent.

"Your patrons have already begun to arrive," Phillipe said.

"Who are these people, and how do they even know about the auction?"

"The gallery's been advertising the event for a few months now," Phillipe replied. "Buyers up and down the west coast are showing serious interest. I suspect your debut will be a smashing success."

With that, he walked away.

"Tada," I squeaked.

"Is it too late to change my mind and be mad at you?" Spike teased.

"Nope, sorry. You locked in your answer. Now, come on, let's get you changed."

"Changed?" Spike furrowed his brow. "Into what?"

"Gemma called in a favor from a designer friend of hers, and had a suit tailored for you. Franco had to calculate your size based on some clothes I stole from you, and pictures of you in my phone. He said if you need any alterations, we can ship the suit back to him in Milan and he'll take care of it."

"Milan, Italy? Wait a minute. Is Gemma's friend Franco Garavaglia?"

"I think so. That sounds right. Do you know him?"

Spike looked stunned. "He's one of the top designers in men's fashion."

"Sounds like the kind of people Gemma's friends with," I said.

"Baby, a custom Franco Garavaglia suit costs seventy-five thousand dollars."

"You'd better not spill mustard on it, then," I said, leading him into the back room.

Spike undressed and I must confess I found it agonizingly difficult to make him redress.

"Baby?"

It took me a second to respond. "Um, yes?"

He chuckled as he glanced around the room. "You know, the door's locked and there are no cameras in here."

I met his eyes. "And?"

"And, you're wearing a skirt."

"Jesse." I bit my lip. "There's a building full of people out there."

He advanced on me, slipping a hand between my legs. "Then we better be very, very quiet."

I mewed as he ripped my panties from my body and dropped them on the floor. "Spike, I need those."

"No, you don't. I want access to your pussy all night."

"Oh my..." I swallowed. "People are going to wonder

why I'm walking funny."

He grinned, leaning down close, nose-to-nose. "I don't give a fuck."

He kissed me as two fingers slid inside, his thumb connecting with my clit and then he was lifting me, anchoring my back to the wall.

"This is gonna be quick, Trixie."

"I'm ready," I panted out.

He buried his dick inside of me and I gasped as his girth filled me. Sliding a hand under my shirt and bra, he cupped my breast and rolled my nipple between his fingers as he slammed into me, careful not to bang me against the wall too hard. I wrapped my legs around his waist and my arms around his neck and held myself steady, trying my hardest not to cry out at the sensations swamping me. Sex just got better and better with him, and knowing there were people right outside just seemed to make it even more exciting.

An orgasm washed over me and I couldn't stop myself from sinking my teeth into his shoulder as my walls contracted around him. Spike wasn't far behind me and he held me against the wall for a few seconds as we both came down.

"Wow," I whispered.

"Wow, indeed." He lowered me to the ground, pulling the handkerchief from his new jacket pocket, and helping me clean up before we got dressed.

Spike's naked body was, without a doubt, the best thing I'd ever seen, but him in the Garavaglia suit was a close second.

"How do I look?" he asked, straightening his tie.

"Edible," I replied.

He chuckled, snagging my panties and the handkerchief off the floor, and shoving them in the pocket of his pants.

I bit my lip, suddenly horny all over again before motioning to the box on the table. "He sent shoes as well."

"Remind me to give Gemma a great big hug for all of this," he said, sliding the beautiful Italian leather shoes on.

"You will do nothing of the sort. Gemma is a man magnet, and I'm not gonna let her steal you away from me and buy your love by giving you pretty things."

"But have you seen the shoes?" he asked with a grin.

"You look absolutely amazing."

Spike leaned down and kissed me. "This is all because of you, baby. All of these people that have rallied around me tonight. They're all here because you made it happen. I'm in a suit that costs as much as a car because of you. People who care about art and have bank accounts are looking at my stuff right now, because of you. This is by far, the most beautiful thing anyone has ever done for me, and that's because you are the most beautiful person I've ever met. Inside and out, and I knew it from the very moment we first met. I don't know if I believe in gods, or divine plans, or if we're all part of some random chain of cosmic events hurtling through spacetime by chance. But I do know that I will always be thankful to who or whatever put you into my life."

He kissed me again. The kind of kiss you never want to break. The kind of kiss that can only be given out of pure love.

"One more thing," Spike said, grabbing his jacket from the back of a chair, and removing something from the inside pocket.

"What is it? You know how bad I am with surprises."

"Hopefully, you like this one," Spike said, before dropping to one knee. "Trixie, I—"

"Yes!" I shouted, bursting into tears. "Yes. I accept, I do, yes."

Spike laughed. "I think the 'I do' part comes a little later, baby, but I'll take it."

He took my hand and placed the most gorgeous ring I could have ever imagined on my hand. "It's...perfect. How did you...?"

"You're not the only one to have Gemma as a resource," he replied. "Don't worry, I paid for it, but she helped me pick it out for you."

"I can't believe you," I said, slapping Spike's chest. "This night is supposed to be all about you, and you go and make an engaged woman out of me."

"Hey, I'm engaged too, ya know."

"Shall we, then?" I asked.

Spike offered his arm and led us back into the gallery. Our lives together, only just beginning.

Trixie

Three months later...

I SET THE stick on the side of the sink then washed and dried my hands as I waited for the results. Spike was in the kitchen, making me a cup of ginger tea, hoping it would help with the sudden nausea I'd been experiencing over the past few days.

Gina, however, had insisted on me taking a pregnancy test despite the fact I'd been on the Pill pretty much since Spike and I had started consummating our relationship. Once he'd gotten a clean bill of health, we'd stopped using condoms, and it had given my contraceptive enough time to kick-in, so to speak, and I'd found that I'd had next to no adverse side effects…well, except maybe pregnancy. Of course, we wouldn't care if that were the case. We were settled and in love, planning a November wedding which would still all work, I might just have to change my dress.

After the gallery night, which ended with Spike almost selling out and *Modern Art Today* reporting that, "Kane has a future as one of the brightest new stars in the world of modern sculpture," we'd come back to the condo and crashed for two straight days.

And after that, I never slept alone. Spike moved his things in and we'd been inseparable ever since. I'd met with Gemma's attorney suing my old employer, and the second she'd sent the letter with all the evidence, we hadn't even needed to file. They offered me a settlement of almost one-million dollars.

I took it. It meant I could pay Ropes back the money he'd shelled out for my father and put the rest in the bank while Spike and I looked for a place to buy. The plan was to stay here for a while because, one, it was in a prime location and there really was no reason to leave quickly, and two, it meant we could take our time and find exactly what we wanted with no pressure. All I knew for sure was that I wanted to be close to Mattias and Ronnie and their cherub of a little girl because, oh my word, she was the cutest thing on the planet, and I wanted our kids to grow up together.

I'd had a minor panic attack when Spike filled me in on the events after the fight and how Edison tried to cheat him out of the money. In the end, Edison had been successfully 'persuaded' to make good on Spike's winnings from the fight and Spike put his purse into a college account for our future kids, so financially we were secure enough to continue to pursue our dreams.

"Trixie?" Spike called, his voice close.

"In here, honey."

"You throwing up again?"

"No," I breathed out, glancing down at the two pink lines on the stick.

"What's goin' on?"

"Well, my love, you're going to be a daddy."

His face lit up. "Yeah?"

"Yes."

He wrapped his arms around my waist and lifted me off my feet before hissing out, "Oh, shit, sorry," setting me on the ground again.

"I'm fine, honey. Picking me up isn't going to hurt me or the baby."

Although, my parents had moved away and they did little to foster any kind of a relationship, I did what I could to reach out on occasion. I tried to keep a healthy boundary so that when they didn't respond, it no longer broke my heart. I had Spike, I had my brothers, and I had the club. I also had my own personal relationship with God, which I tried to keep separate from the trauma and the gaslighting I'd experienced throughout my life.

"Come and sit down. From now on, you do nothing," he said, taking my hand and leading me out to the great room.

"You barely let me do anything now."

"Well, now neither of you are going to barely do anything."

I laughed. "You're going to create monsters."

"I can live with that."

I let out a mock growl which really sounded more like a cat purring.

Spike chuckled. "Come on baby, I'll pop some popcorn and we'll watch Joe Versus the Volcano."

"Yes!" I exclaimed.

And we lived happily ever after.

RUM-SPRING-A

2oz Light Rum
4oz 7up (or Sprite)
½ TSP Grenadine
Maraschino Cherry

Pour over ice and stir!

USA Today Bestselling Author Jack Davenport is a true romantic at heart, but he has a rebel's soul. His writing is passionate, energetic, and often fueled by his true life, fiery romance with author wife, Piper Davenport.

Twenty-five years as a professional musician lends a unique perspective into the world of rock stars, while his outlaw upbringing gives an authenticity to his MC series.

Like Jack's FB page and get to know him!
(www.facebook.com/jackdavenportauthor)

Made in the USA
Columbia, SC
24 March 2023

14253787R00135